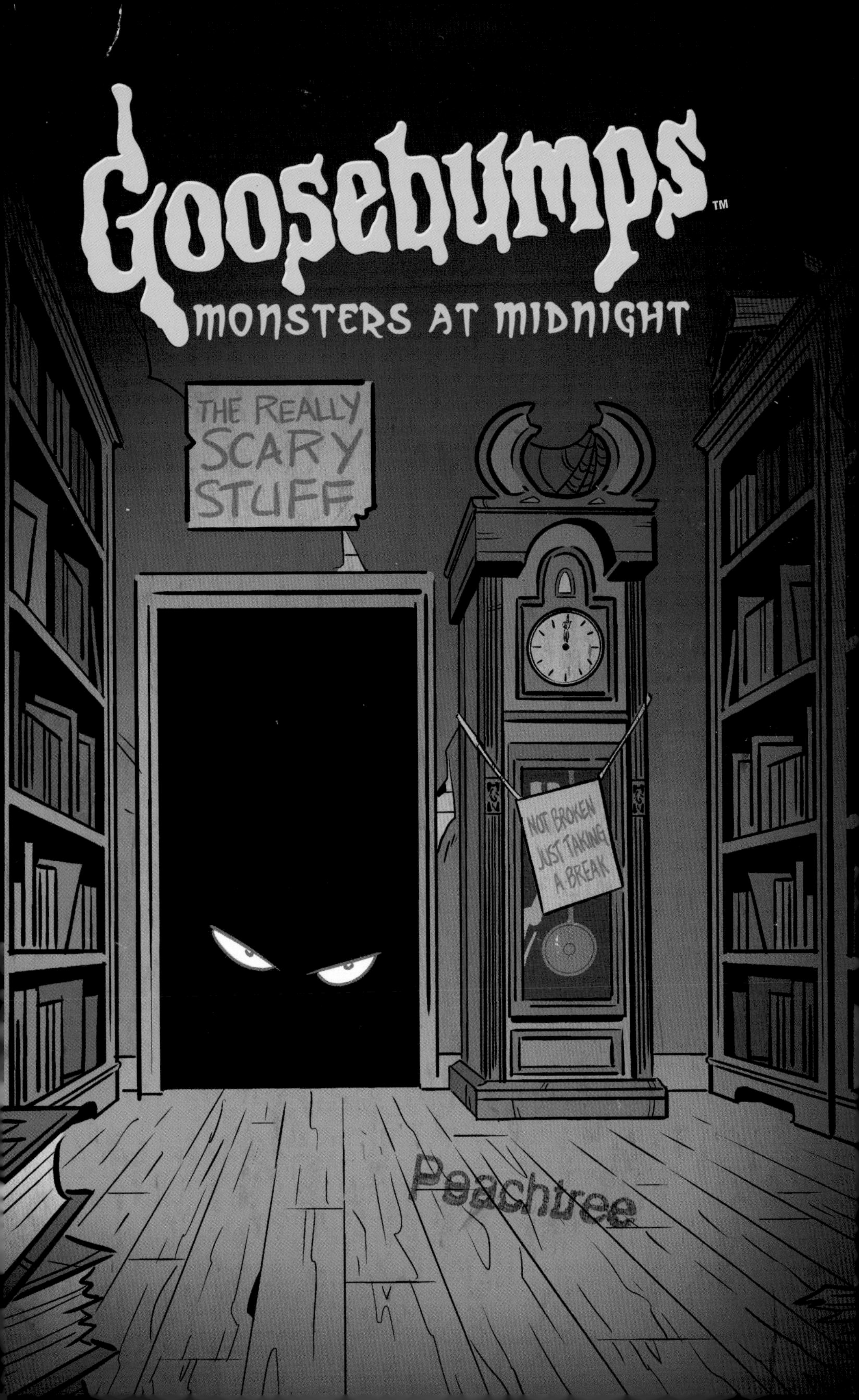
Goosebumps™
MONSTERS AT MIDNIGHT
THE REALLY SCARY STUFF
NOT BROKEN JUST TAKING A BREAK
Peachtree

Become our fan on Facebook **facebook.com/idwpublishing**
Follow us on Twitter **@idwpublishing**
Subscribe to us on YouTube **youtube.com/idwpublishing**
See what's new on Tumblr **tumblr.idwpublishing.com**
Check us out on Instagram **instagram.com/idwpublishing**

Greg Goldstein, President & Publisher
Robbie Robbins, EVP & Sr. Art Director
Chris Ryall, Chief Creative Officer & Editor-in-Chief
Matthew Ruzicka, CPA, Chief Financial Officer
David Hedgecock, Associate Publisher
Laurie Windrow, Senior Vice President of Sales & Marketing
Lorelei Bunjes, VP of Digital Services
Eric Moss, Sr. Director, Licensing & Business Development

Ted Adams, Founder & CEO of IDW Media Holdings

ISBN: 978-1-68405-155-7 21 20 19 18 2 3 4 5

Originally published as GOOSEBUMPS: MONSTERS AT MIDNIGHT issues #1–3.

Special thanks to R.L. Stine.

For international rights, contact licensing@idwpublishing.com

SCHOLASTIC

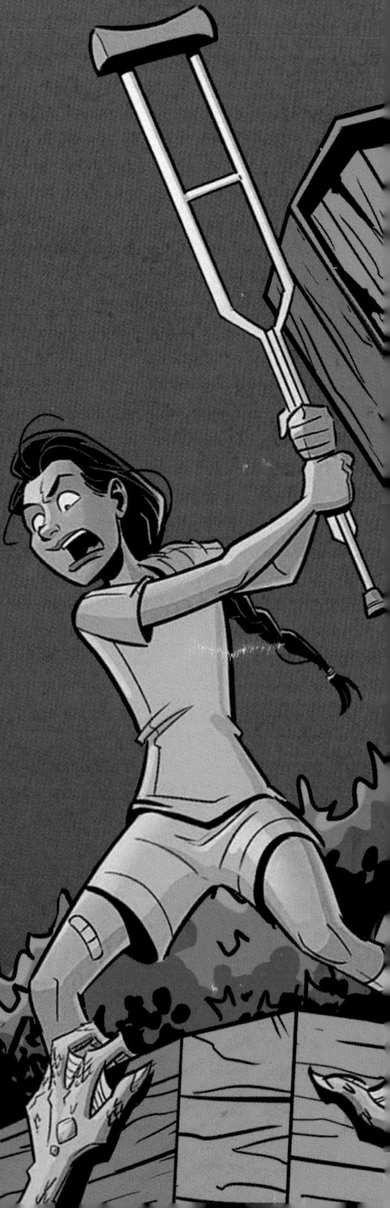

WRITER
JEREMY LAMBERT

ARTIST
CHRIS FENOGLIO

COLORISTS
CHRIS FENOGLIO AND
BRITTANY PEER

LETTERER
CHRISTA MIESNER

SERIES ASSISTANT EDITOR
CHASE MAROTZ

SERIES EDITOR
SARAH GAYDOS

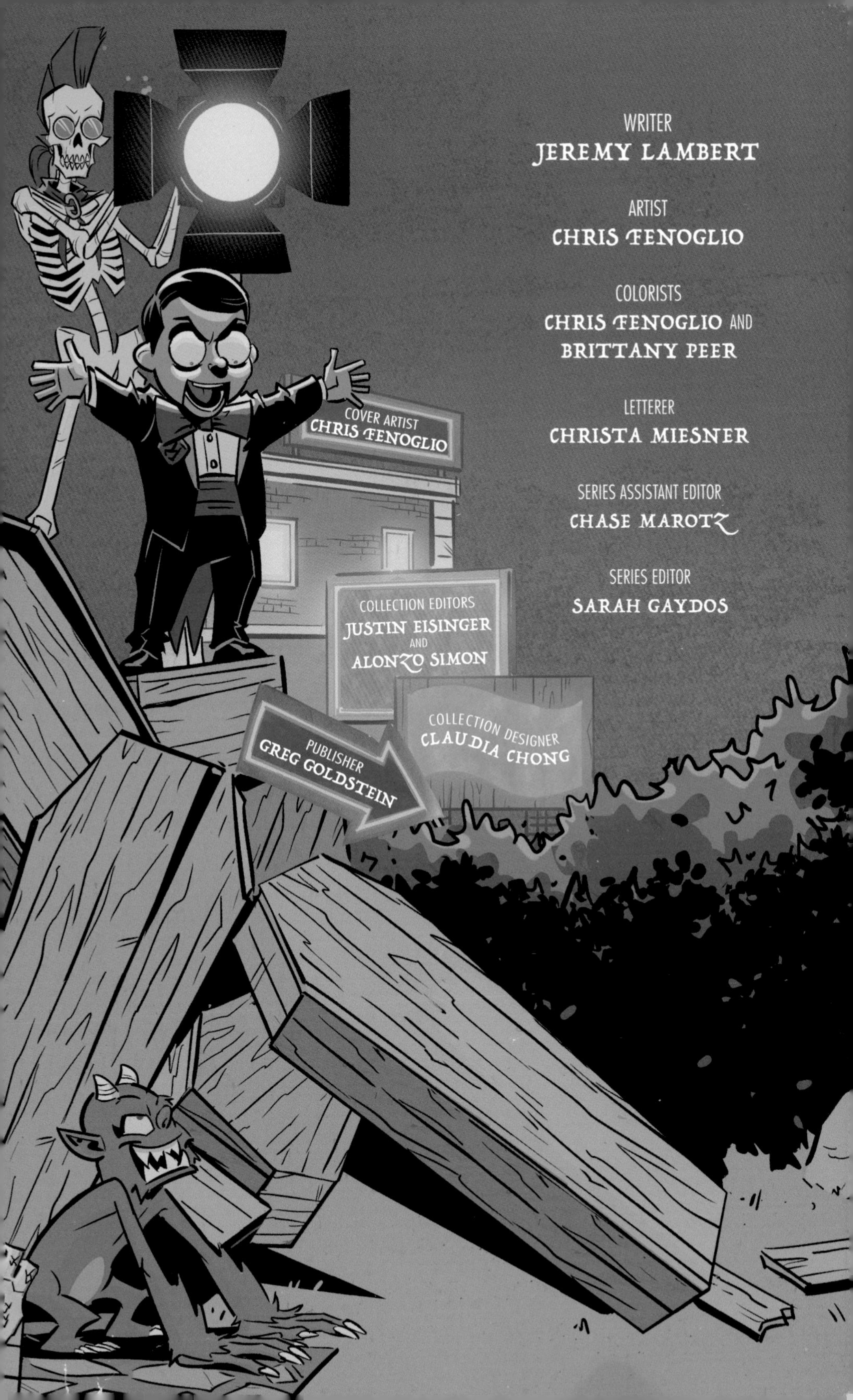
COVER ARTIST
CHRIS FENOGLIO
COLLECTION EDITORS
JUSTIN EISINGER
AND
ALONZO SIMON
PUBLISHER
GREG GOLDSTEIN
COLLECTION DESIGNER
CLAUDIA CHONG

[redacted]

The gates are open. Slappy the living dummy and his evil cohorts await. You've just picked up a Fast Pass to all the frights and surprises the park can offer. Listen, guys, this isn't the Magic Kingdom—unless your idea of magic time is to be screaming your head off in terror.

How exciting it is for me to see my evil theme park come to life on the pages of these comics! And do you know what's even more exciting than seeing my characters come to life? It's seeing the new directions the writers and artists take with my work.

These are new *Goosebumps* stories—new to *me*, too.

New kids, new settings, new dangers, and new surprises. I can't tell you what a pleasure it is for me to see artists and writers take a fresh approach and put their own imprint on the *Goosebumps* world. It's the first time I can read a *Goosebumps* story and enjoy the twists and surprises along with everyone else!

As a kid back in Ohio, I was obsessed with comics, as were my friends. We carried stacks of them everywhere we went. We spent whole summers reading them, then trading them, and reading some more.

My parents bought me one-year subscriptions to a bunch of comics so I wouldn't miss a single issue. Every afternoon, I would run to the mailbox to see if a new comic book had arrived.

I had wide-ranging tastes as a kid. I remember I subscribed to *Looney Tunes* and *Scrooge McDuck, Woody Woodpecker* and *Andy Panda,* as well as *Roy Rogers, The Lone Ranger* and *Dick Tracy.*

When a comic book arrived, I would carry it to my room, or to the shady spot under the oak tree in our front yard, and I would read it as slowly as I could. I always wanted to make it last.

Yes, this is the kind of reading excitement that only a kid—or a true comic-book freak—can enjoy. I think about it each time I start a new *Goosebumps* book and hope I can impart that same reading joy.

If you are new to *Goosebumps*—or if you are a *Goosebumps* fan, I hope you will find that same excitement in this terrific collection of new *Goosebumps* adventures.

R.L. Stine

JANUARY 2018

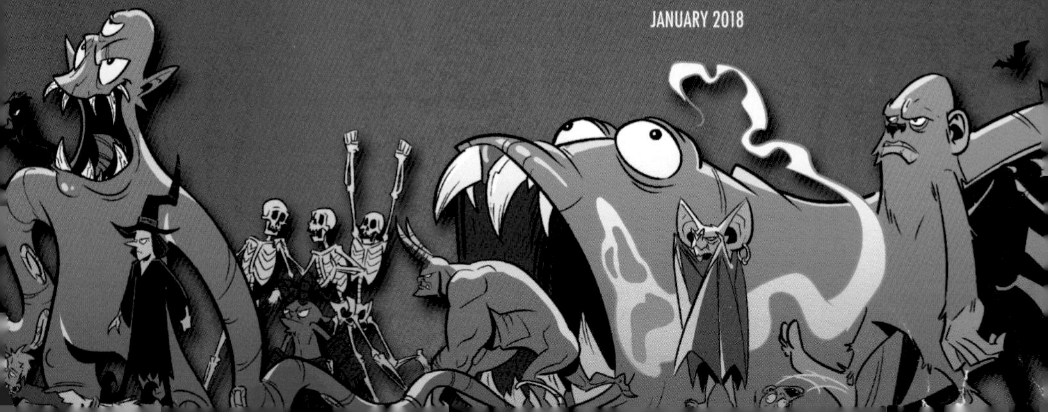

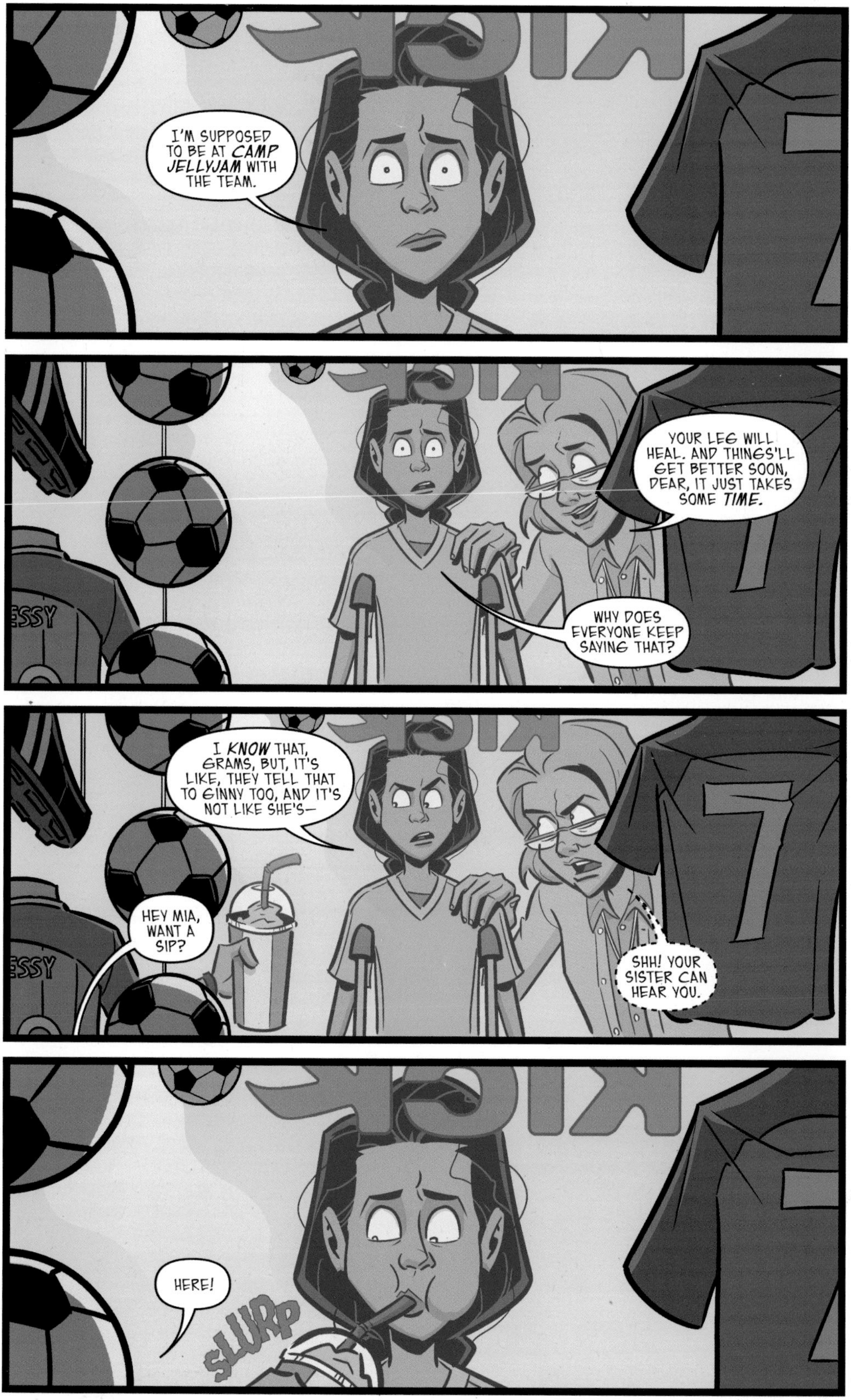
I'M SUPPOSED TO BE AT CAMP JELLYJAM WITH THE TEAM.
YOUR LEG WILL HEAL. AND THINGS'LL GET BETTER SOON, DEAR, IT JUST TAKES SOME TIME.
WHY DOES EVERYONE KEEP SAYING THAT?
ESSY
I KNOW THAT, GRAMS, BUT, IT'S LIKE, THEY TELL THAT TO GINNY TOO, AND IT'S NOT LIKE SHE'S—
HEY MIA, WANT A SIP?
SHH! YOUR SISTER CAN HEAR YOU.
7
HERE!
SLURP

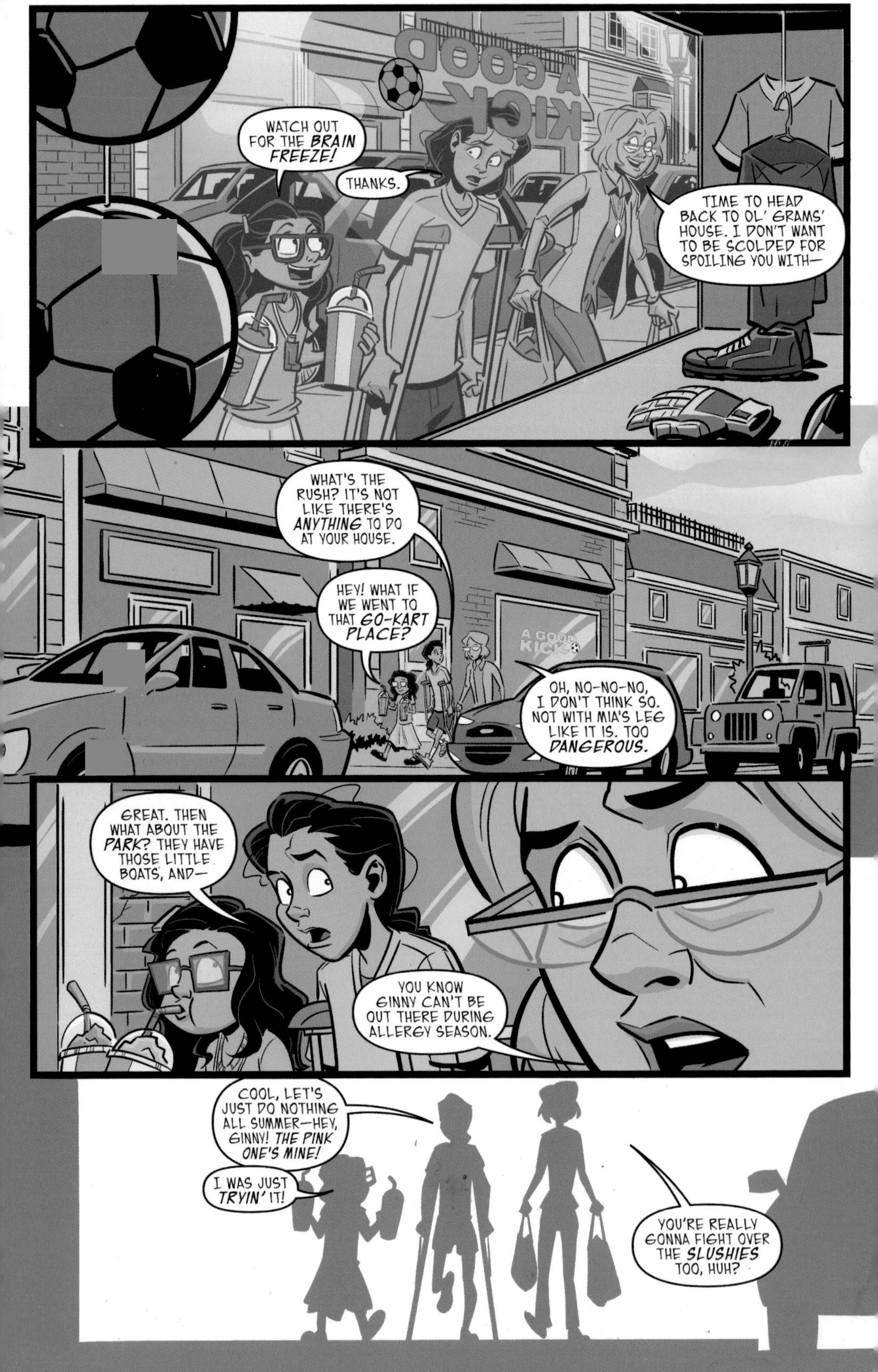
A GOOD KICK
WATCH OUT FOR THE BRAIN FREEZE!
THANKS.
TIME TO HEAD BACK TO OL' GRAMS' HOUSE. I DON'T WANT TO BE SCOLDED FOR SPOILING YOU WITH—
WHAT'S THE RUSH? IT'S NOT LIKE THERE'S ANYTHING TO DO AT YOUR HOUSE.
HEY! WHAT IF WE WENT TO THAT GO-KART PLACE?
A GOOD KICK
OH, NO-NO-NO, I DON'T THINK SO. NOT WITH MIA'S LEG LIKE IT IS. TOO DANGEROUS.
GREAT. THEN WHAT ABOUT THE PARK? THEY HAVE THOSE LITTLE BOATS, AND—
YOU KNOW GINNY CAN'T BE OUT THERE DURING ALLERGY SEASON.
COOL, LET'S JUST DO NOTHING ALL SUMMER—HEY, GINNY! THE PINK ONE'S MINE!
I WAS JUST TRYIN' IT!
YOU'RE REALLY GONNA FIGHT OVER THE SLUSHIES TOO, HUH?

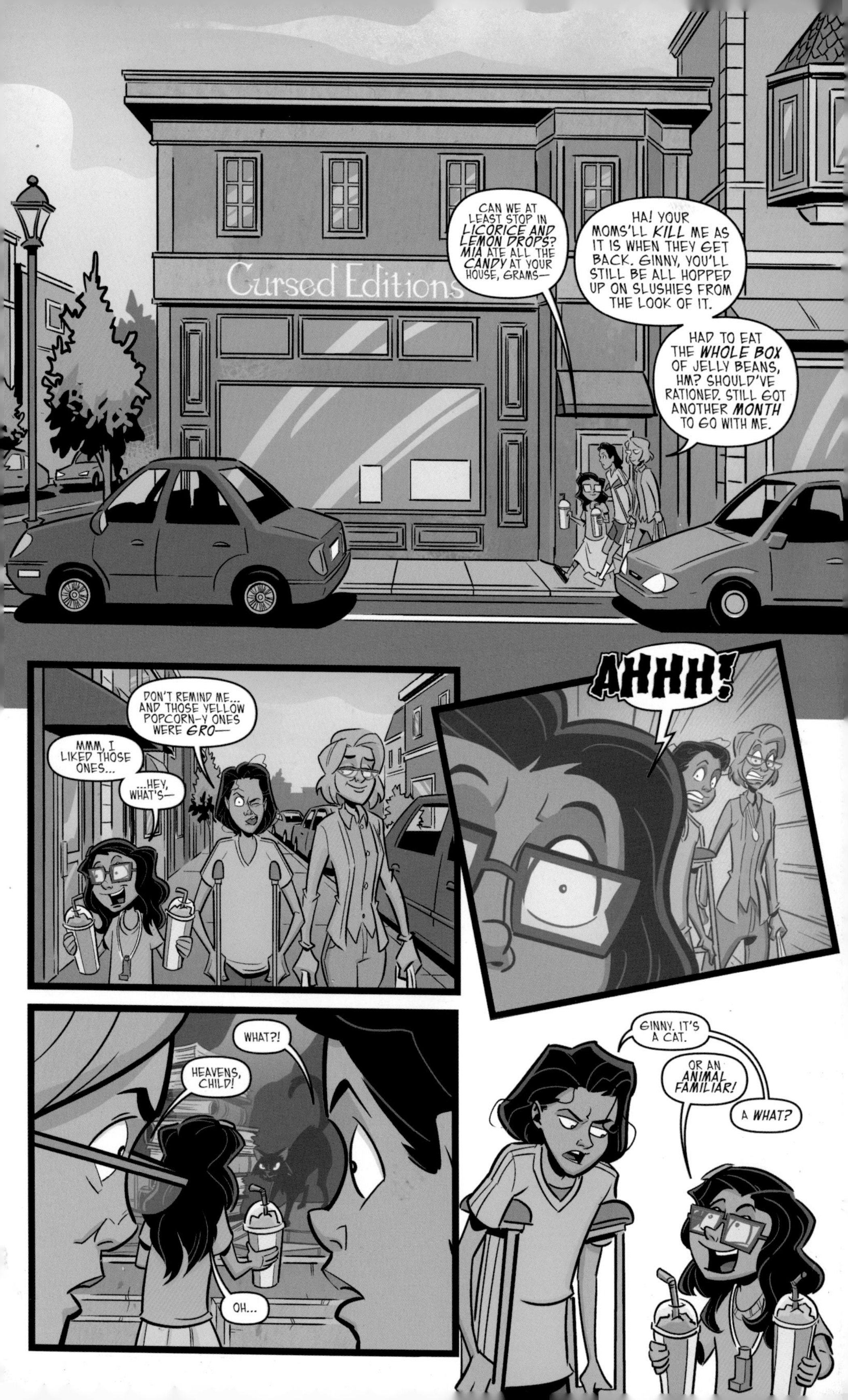
Cursed Editions
CAN WE AT LEAST STOP IN LICORICE AND LEMON DROPS? MIA ATE ALL THE CANDY AT YOUR HOUSE, GRAMS—
HA! YOUR MOMS'LL KILL ME AS IT IS WHEN THEY GET BACK. GINNY, YOU'LL STILL BE ALL HOPPED UP ON SLUSHIES FROM THE LOOK OF IT.
HAD TO EAT THE WHOLE BOX OF JELLY BEANS, HM? SHOULD'VE RATIONED. STILL GOT ANOTHER MONTH TO GO WITH ME.
DON'T REMIND ME... AND THOSE YELLOW POPCORN-Y ONES WERE GRO—
MMM, I LIKED THOSE ONES...
...HEY, WHAT'S—
AHHH!
WHAT?!
HEAVENS, CHILD!
OH...
GINNY. IT'S A CAT.
OR AN ANIMAL FAMILIAR!
A WHAT?

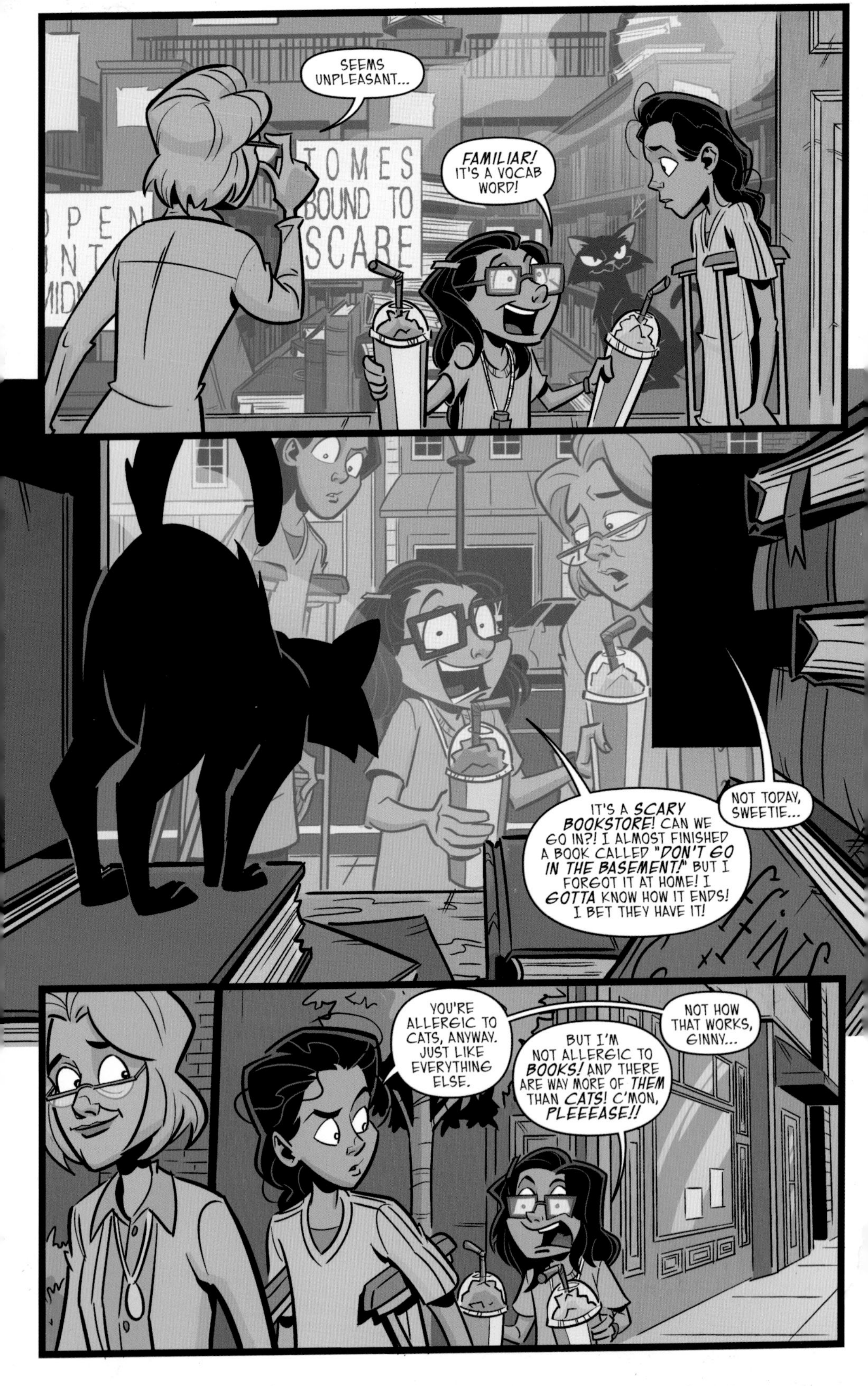
SEEMS UNPLEASANT...
FAMILIAR! IT'S A VOCAB WORD!
TOMES BOUND TO SCARE
OPEN
IT'S A SCARY BOOKSTORE! CAN WE GO IN?! I ALMOST FINISHED A BOOK CALLED "DON'T GO IN THE BASEMENT!" BUT I FORGOT IT AT HOME! I GOTTA KNOW HOW IT ENDS! I BET THEY HAVE IT!
NOT TODAY, SWEETIE...
YOU'RE ALLERGIC TO CATS, ANYWAY. JUST LIKE EVERYTHING ELSE.
BUT I'M NOT ALLERGIC TO BOOKS! AND THERE ARE WAY MORE OF THEM THAN CATS! C'MON, PLEEEASE!!
NOT HOW THAT WORKS, GINNY...

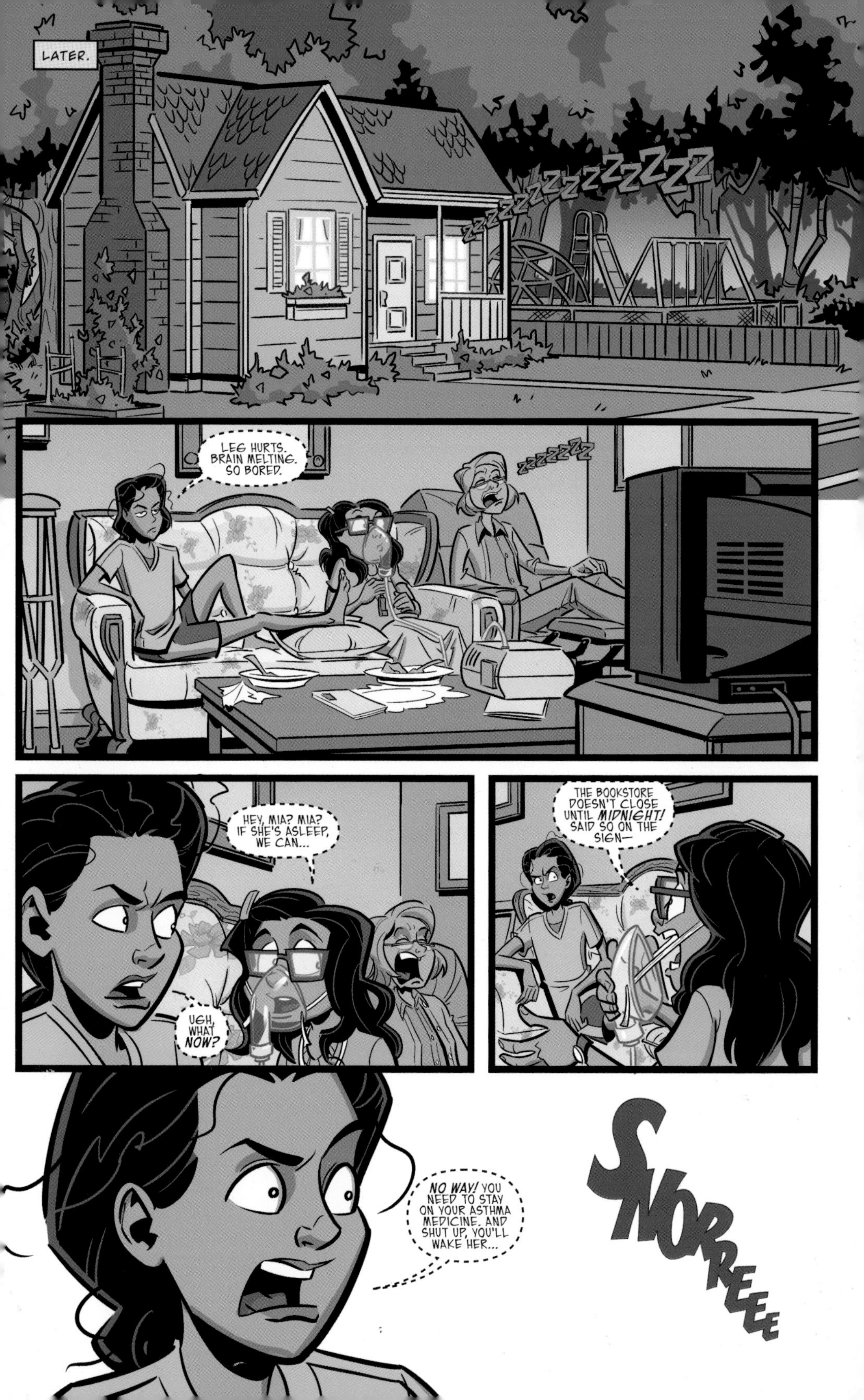
LATER.
ZZZZZZZZZZZ
LEG HURTS. BRAIN MELTING. SO BORED.
ZZZZZZZ
HEY, MIA? MIA? IF SHE'S ASLEEP, WE CAN...
UGH, WHAT NOW?
THE BOOKSTORE DOESN'T CLOSE UNTIL MIDNIGHT! SAID SO ON THE SIGN—
NO WAY! YOU NEED TO STAY ON YOUR ASTHMA MEDICINE. AND SHUT UP, YOU'LL WAKE HER...
SNORREEE

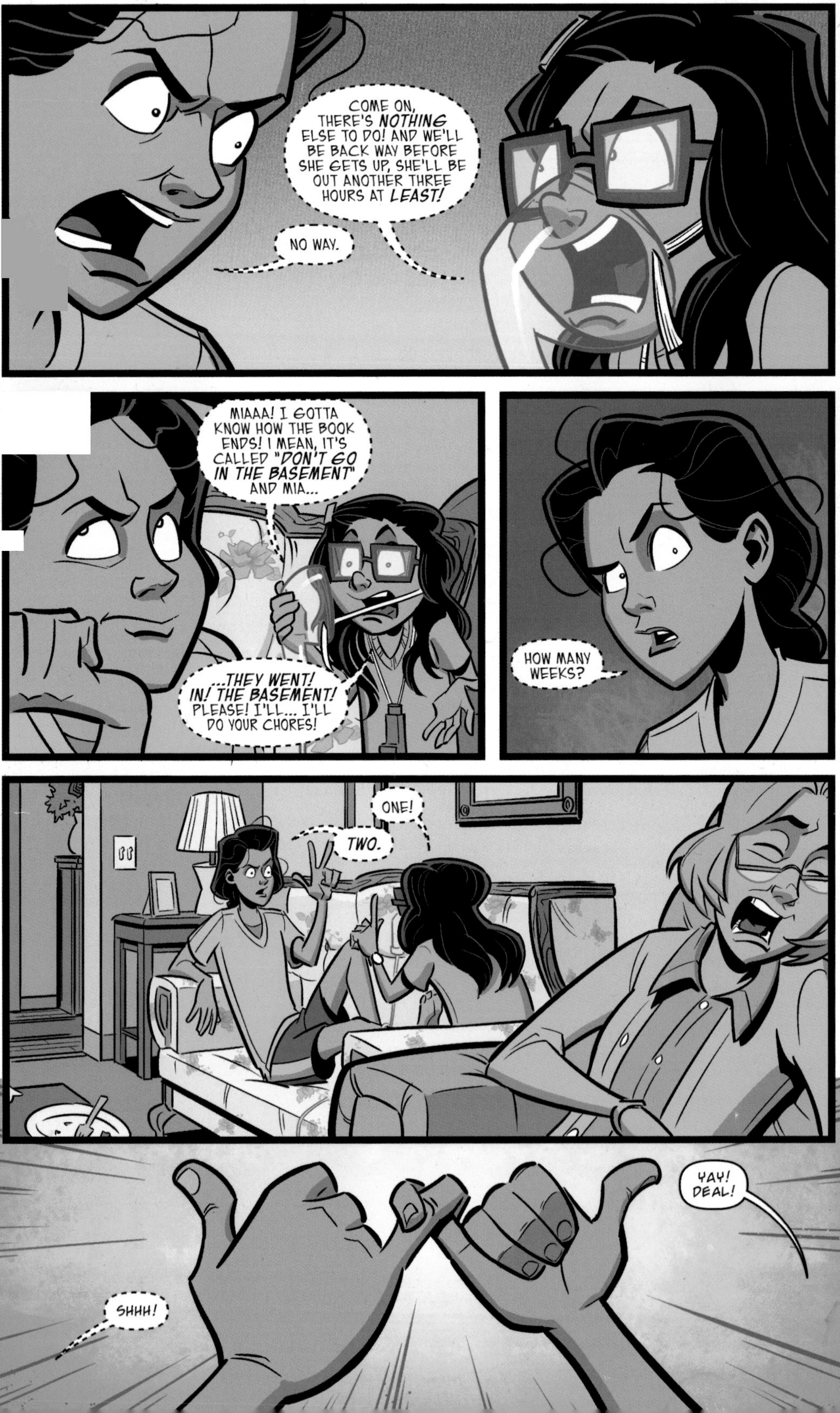
COME ON, THERE'S NOTHING ELSE TO DO! AND WE'LL BE BACK WAY BEFORE SHE GETS UP, SHE'LL BE OUT ANOTHER THREE HOURS AT LEAST!
NO WAY.
MIAAA! I GOTTA KNOW HOW THE BOOK ENDS! I MEAN, IT'S CALLED "DON'T GO IN THE BASEMENT" AND MIA...
...THEY WENT! IN! THE BASEMENT! PLEASE! I'LL... I'LL DO YOUR CHORES!
HOW MANY WEEKS?
ONE!
TWO.
YAY! DEAL!
SHHH!

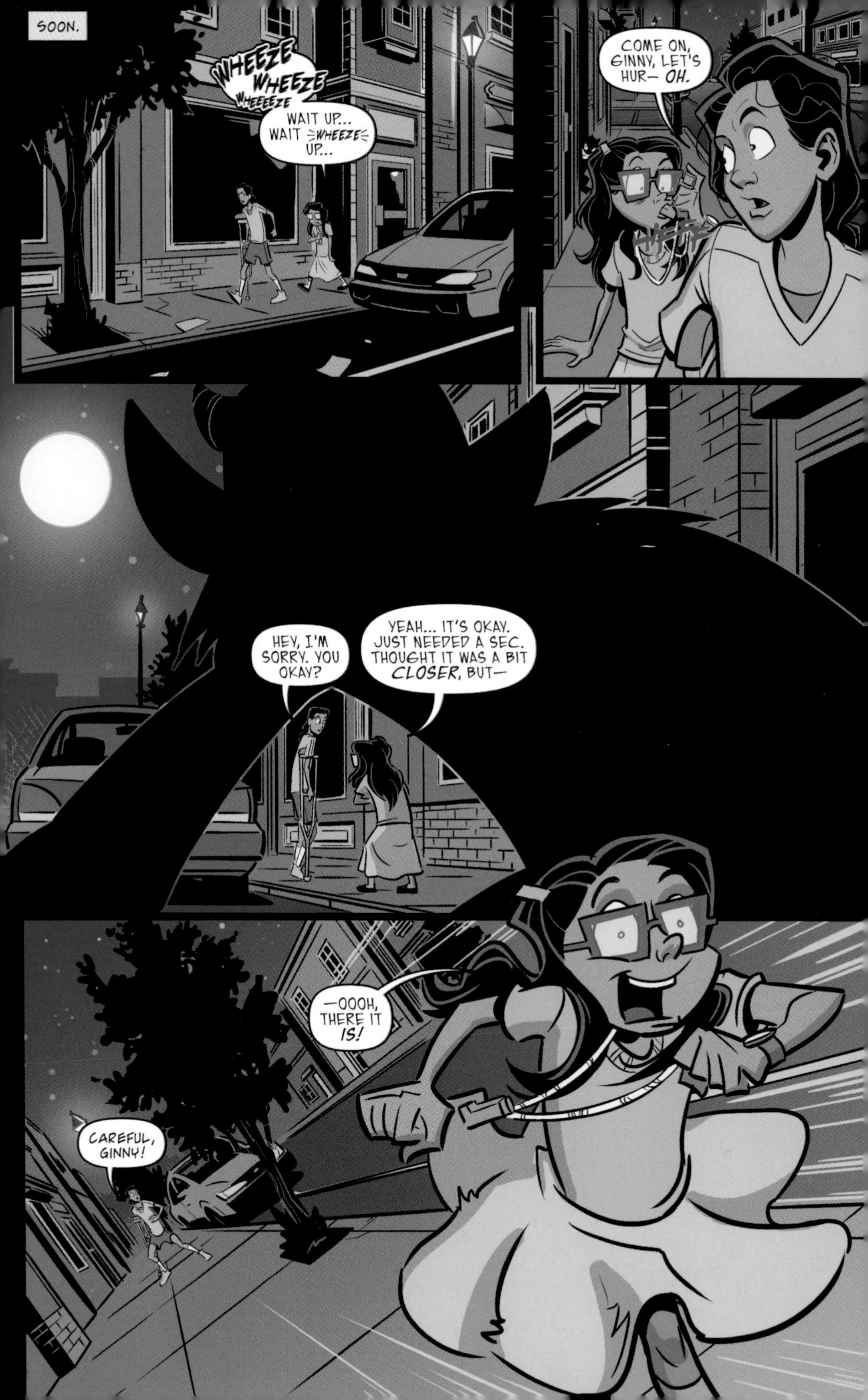
SOON.
WHEEZE WHEEZE WHEEEEZE
WAIT UP... WAIT =WHEEZE= UP...
COME ON, GINNY, LET'S HUR— OH.
HEY, I'M SORRY. YOU OKAY?
YEAH... IT'S OKAY. JUST NEEDED A SEC. THOUGHT IT WAS A BIT CLOSER, BUT—
—OOOH, THERE IT IS!
CAREFUL, GINNY!

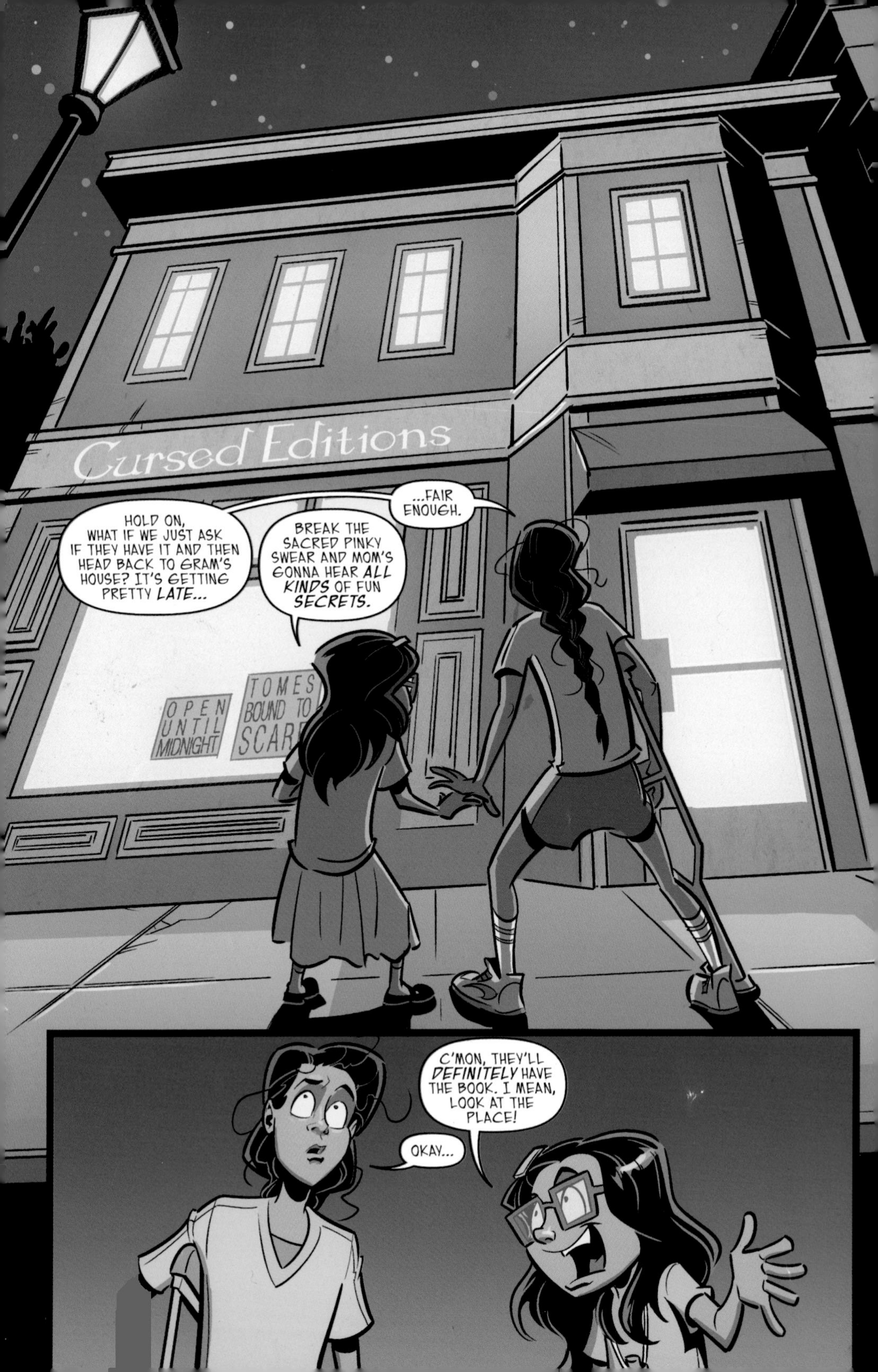
Cursed Editions
HOLD ON, WHAT IF WE JUST ASK IF THEY HAVE IT AND THEN HEAD BACK TO GRAM'S HOUSE? IT'S GETTING PRETTY LATE...
BREAK THE SACRED PINKY SWEAR AND MOM'S GONNA HEAR ALL KINDS OF FUN SECRETS.
...FAIR ENOUGH.
OPEN UNTIL MIDNIGHT
C'MON, THEY'LL DEFINITELY HAVE THE BOOK. I MEAN, LOOK AT THE PLACE!
OKAY...

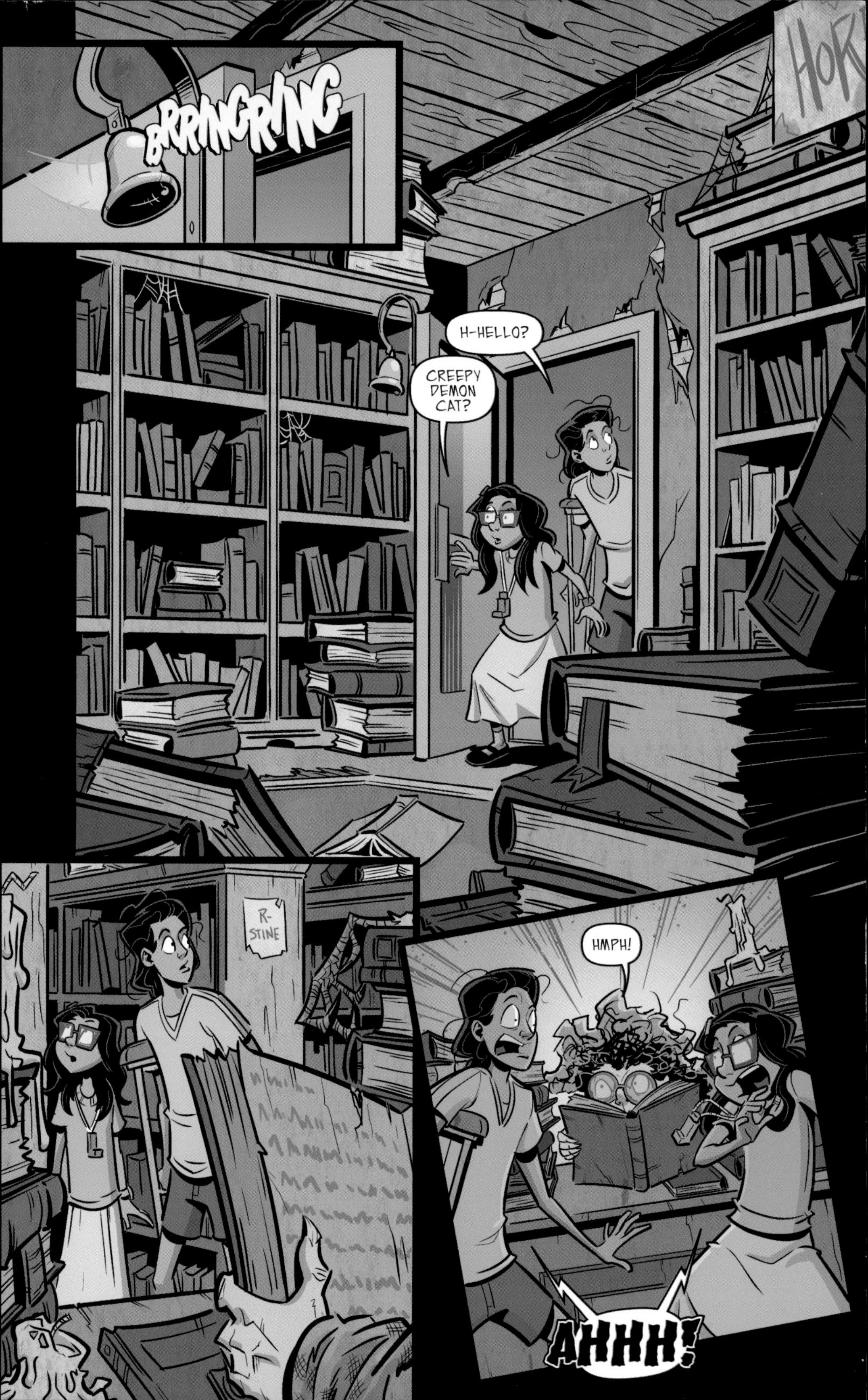
BRRINGRING
H-HELLO?
CREEPY DEMON CAT?
HOR
R-STINE
HMPH!
AHHH!

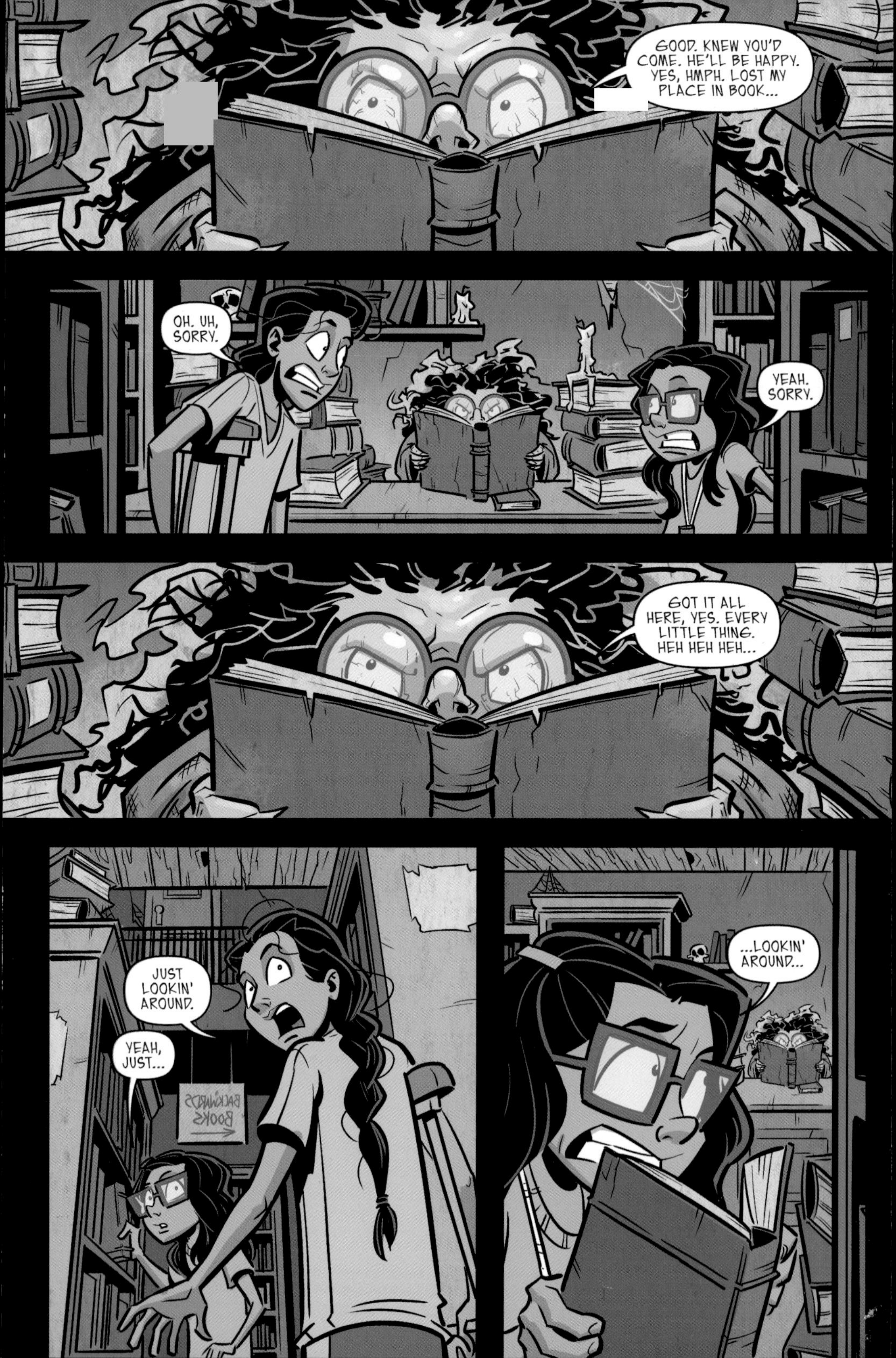
GOOD. KNEW YOU'D COME. HE'LL BE HAPPY. YES, HMPH. LOST MY PLACE IN BOOK...
OH. UH, SORRY.
YEAH. SORRY.
GOT IT ALL HERE, YES. EVERY LITTLE THING. HEH HEH HEH...
JUST LOOKIN' AROUND.
YEAH, JUST...
BACKWARDS BOOKS
...LOOKIN' AROUND...

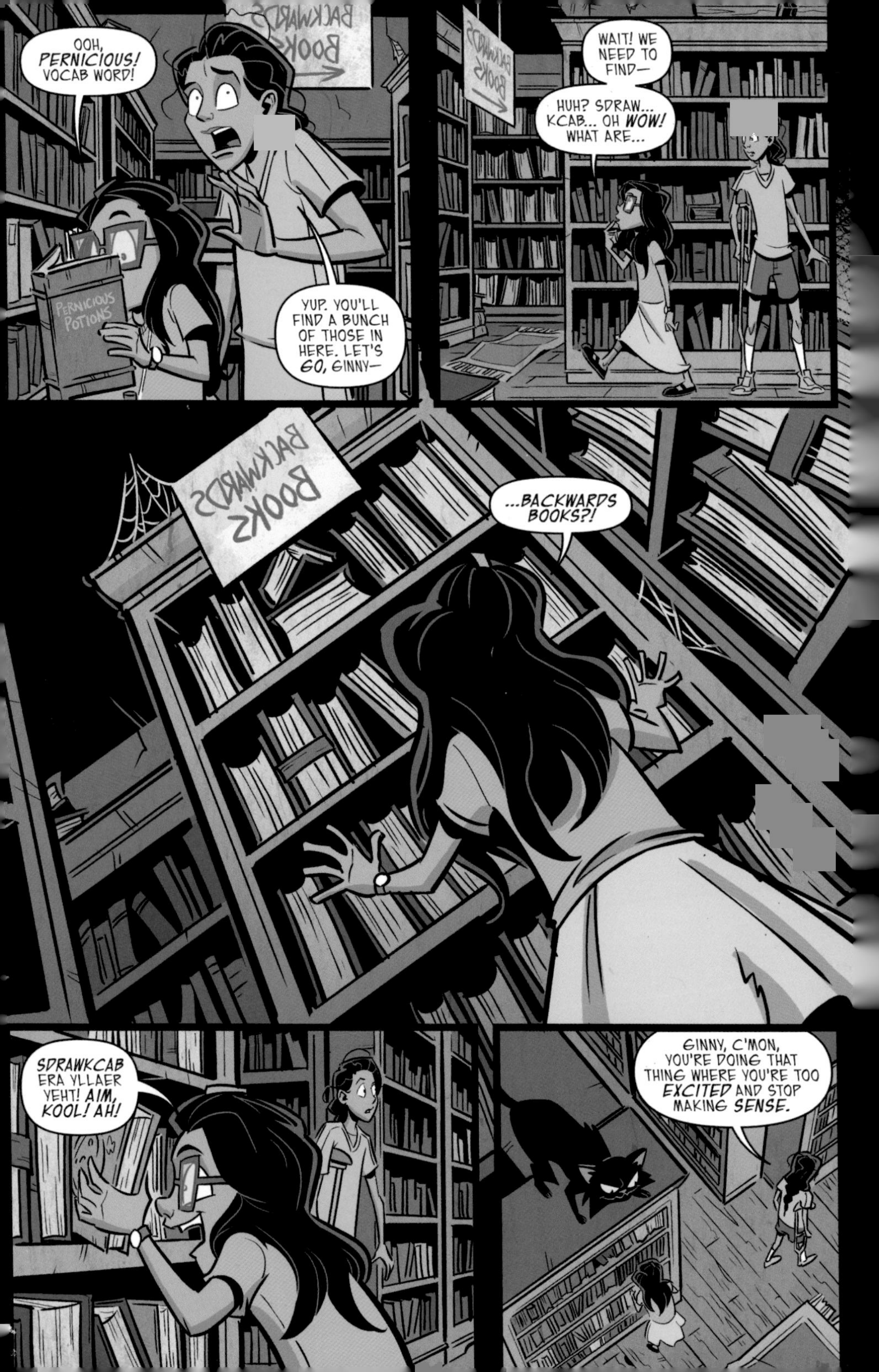
BACKWARDS BOOKS
OOH, PERNICIOUS! VOCAB WORD!
PERNICIOUS POTIONS
YUP. YOU'LL FIND A BUNCH OF THOSE IN HERE. LET'S GO, GINNY—
WAIT! WE NEED TO FIND—
HUH? SDRAW... KCAB... OH WOW! WHAT ARE...
...BACKWARDS BOOKS?!
SDRAWKCAB ERA YLLAER YEHT! AIM, KOOL! AH!
GINNY, C'MON, YOU'RE DOING THAT THING WHERE YOU'RE TOO EXCITED AND STOP MAKING SENSE.

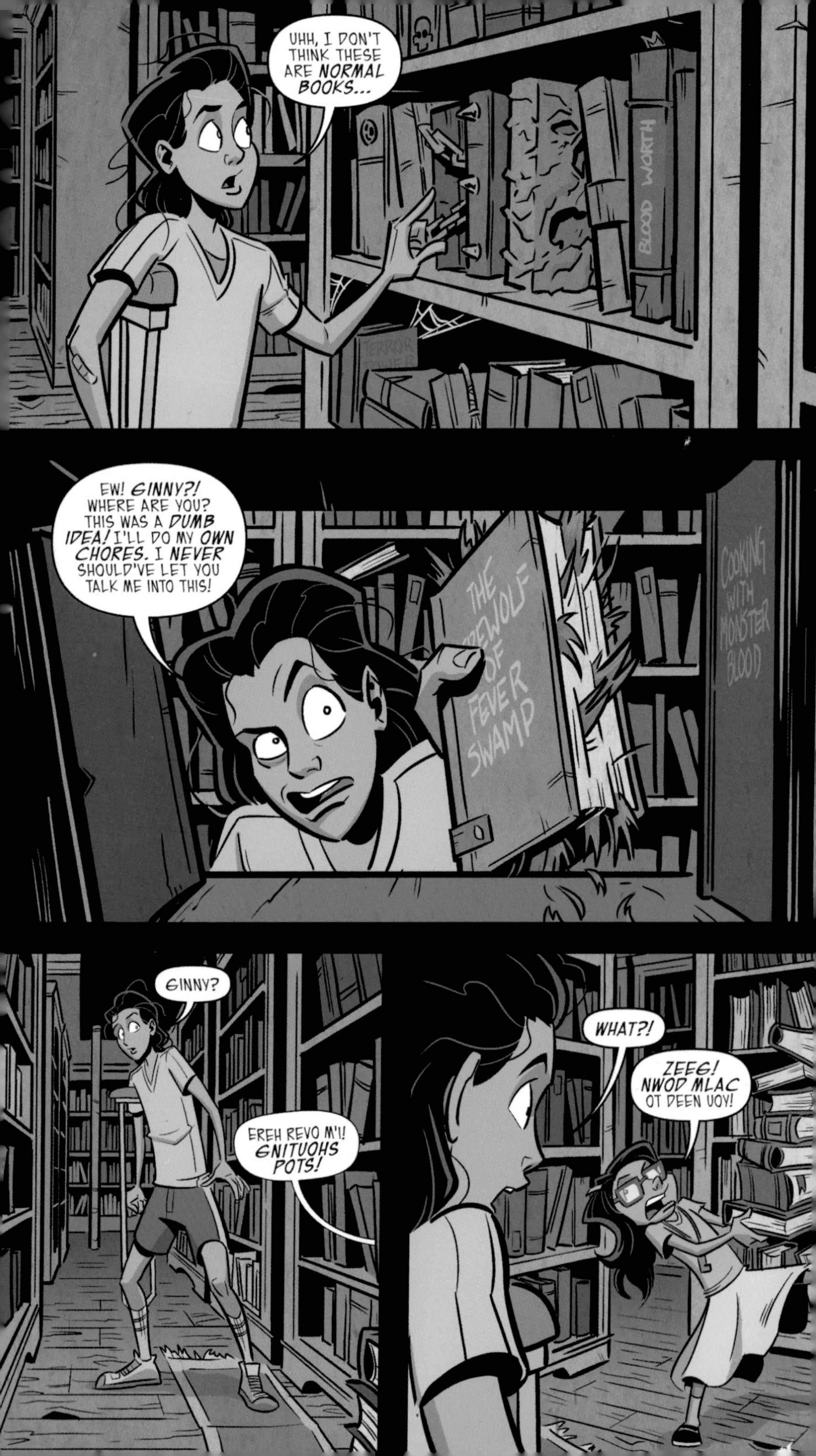
UHH, I DON'T THINK THESE ARE NORMAL BOOKS...
BLOOD WORTH
TERROR TOWER
EW! GINNY?! WHERE ARE YOU? THIS WAS A DUMB IDEA! I'LL DO MY OWN CHORES. I NEVER SHOULD'VE LET YOU TALK ME INTO THIS!
THE ...REWOLF OF FEVER SWAMP
COOKING WITH MONSTER BLOOD
GINNY?
EREH REVO M'I! GNITUOHS POTS!
WHAT?!
ZEEG! NWOD MLAC OT DEEN UOY!

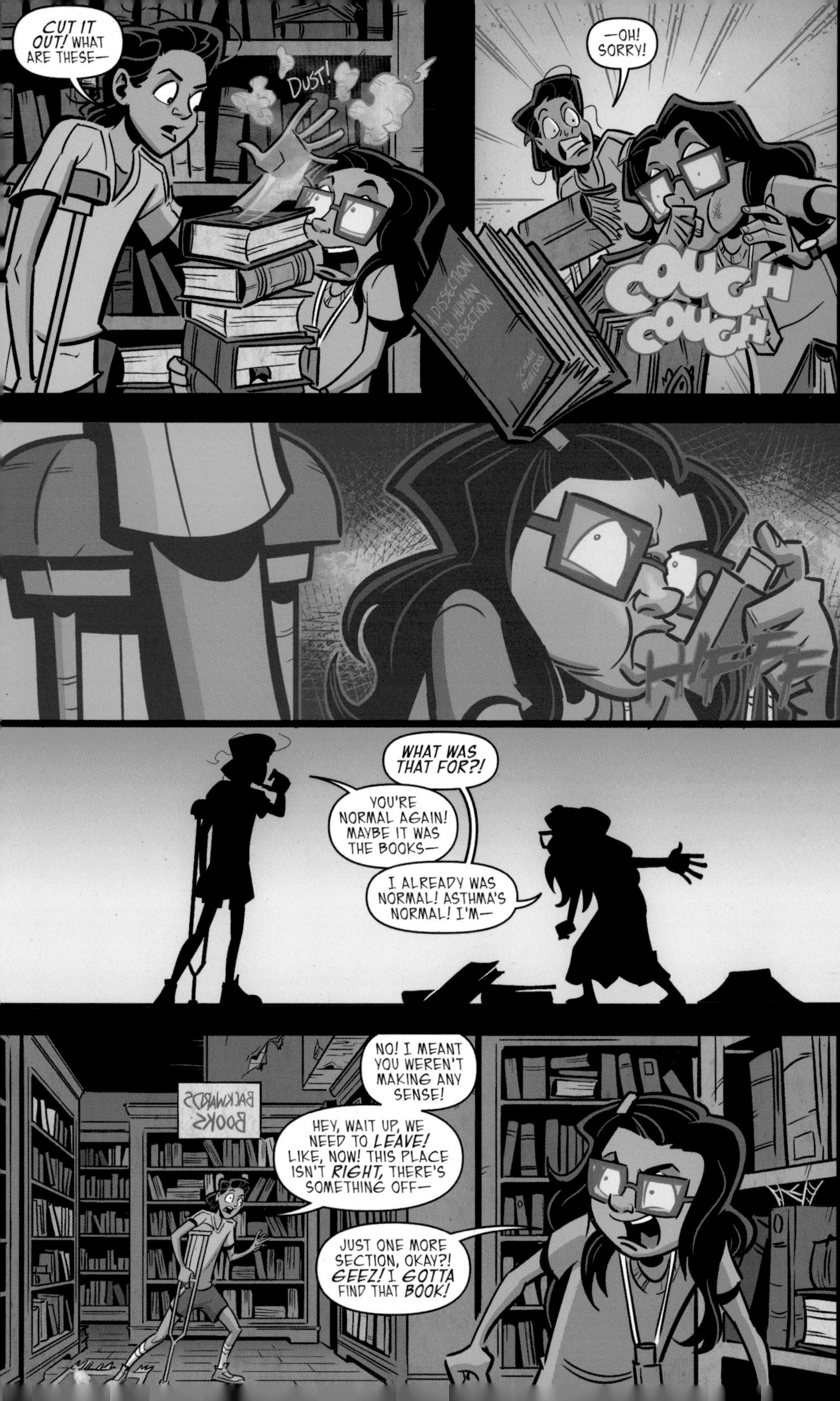
CUT IT OUT! WHAT ARE THESE—
DUST!
—OH! SORRY!
A DISSECTION ON HUMAN DISSECTION
COUGH COUGH
WHAT WAS THAT FOR?!
YOU'RE NORMAL AGAIN! MAYBE IT WAS THE BOOKS—
I ALREADY WAS NORMAL! ASTHMA'S NORMAL! I'M—
NO! I MEANT YOU WEREN'T MAKING ANY SENSE!
BACKWARDS BOOKS
HEY, WAIT UP, WE NEED TO LEAVE! LIKE, NOW! THIS PLACE ISN'T RIGHT, THERE'S SOMETHING OFF—
JUST ONE MORE SECTION, OKAY?! GEEZ! I GOTTA FIND THAT BOOK!

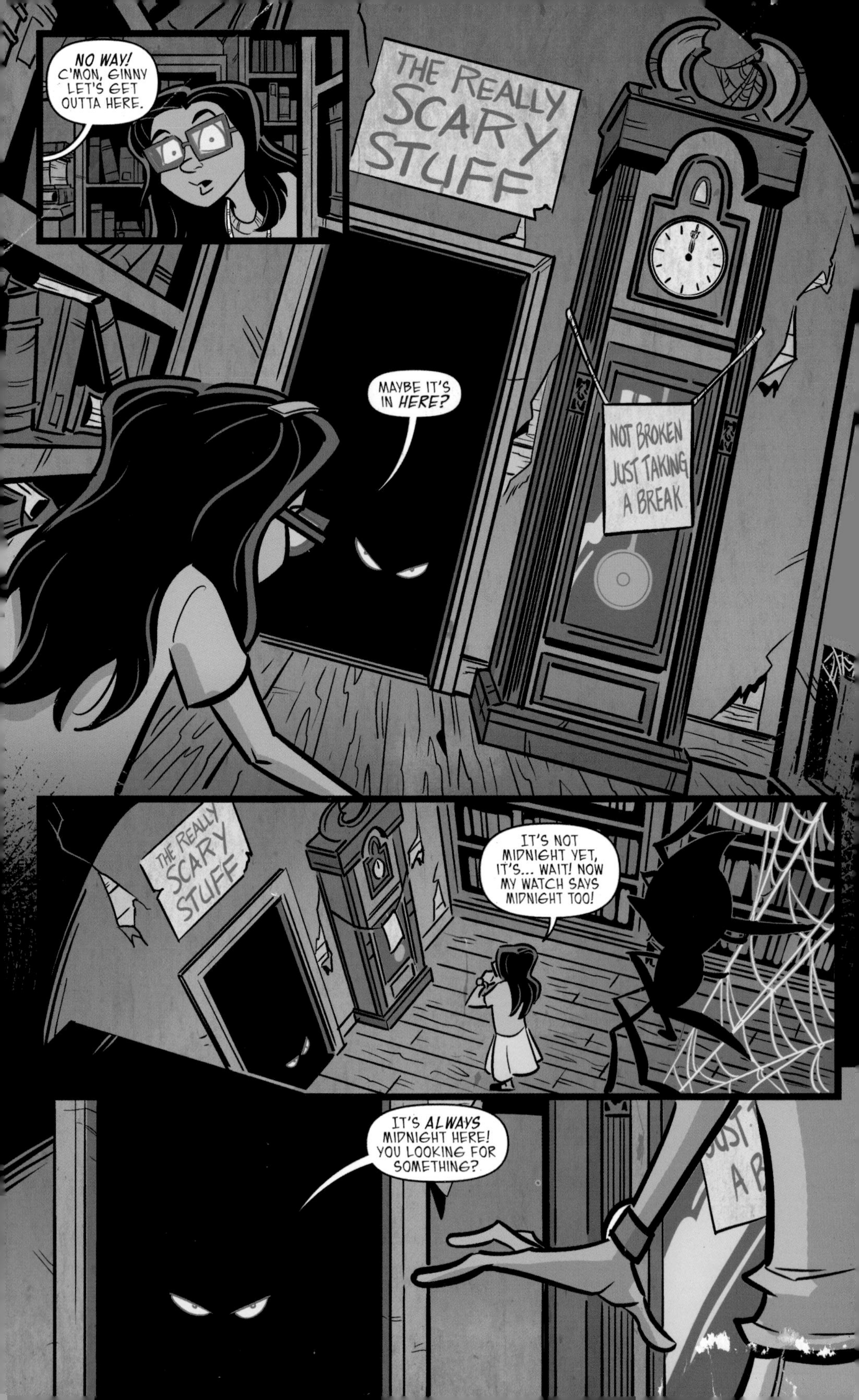
NO WAY! C'MON, GINNY LET'S GET OUTTA HERE.
THE REALLY SCARY STUFF
MAYBE IT'S IN HERE?
NOT BROKEN JUST TAKING A BREAK
THE REALLY SCARY STUFF
IT'S NOT MIDNIGHT YET, IT'S... WAIT! NOW MY WATCH SAYS MIDNIGHT TOO!
IT'S ALWAYS MIDNIGHT HERE! YOU LOOKING FOR SOMETHING?

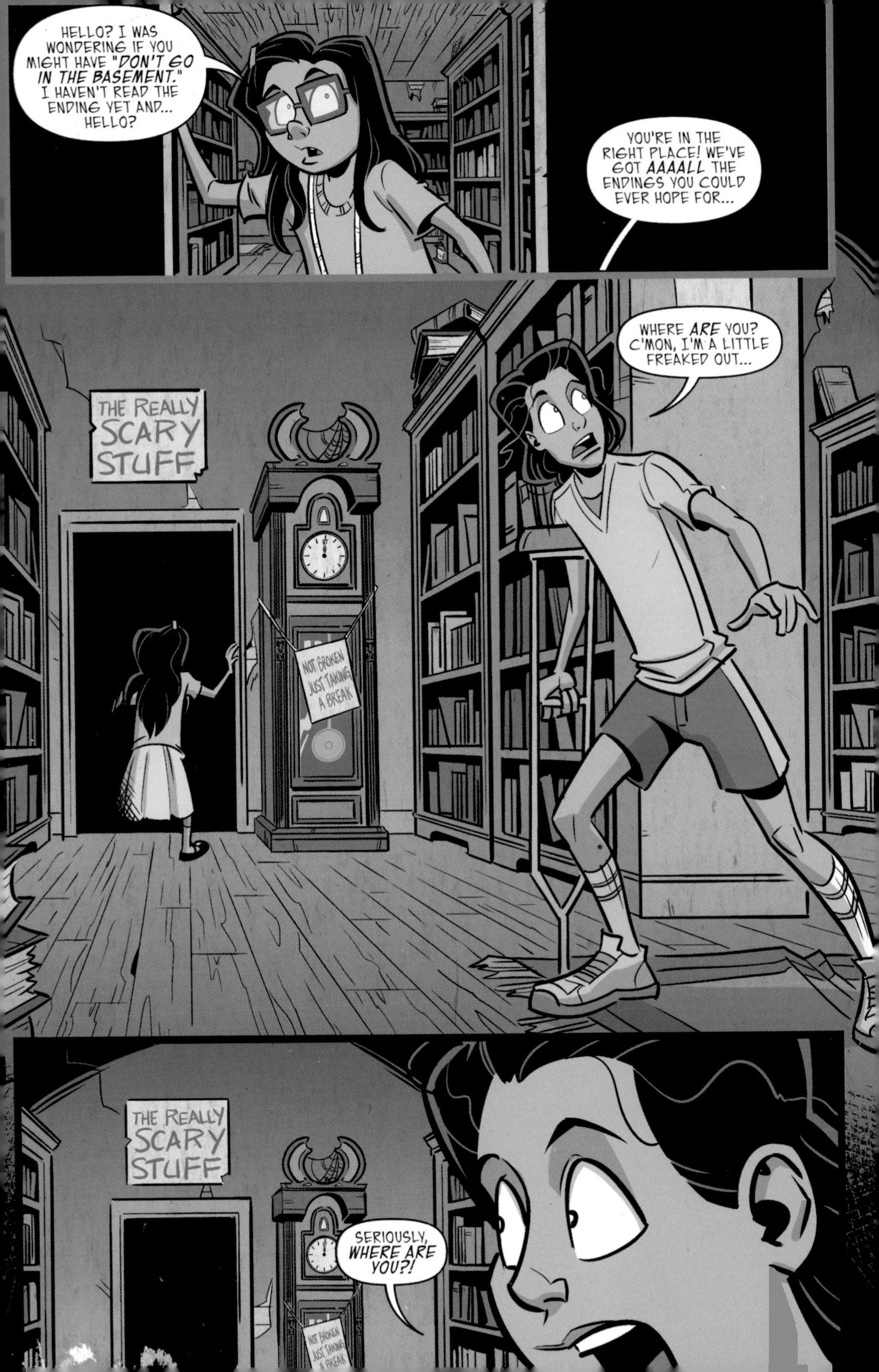
HELLO? I WAS WONDERING IF YOU MIGHT HAVE "DON'T GO IN THE BASEMENT." I HAVEN'T READ THE ENDING YET AND... HELLO?
YOU'RE IN THE RIGHT PLACE! WE'VE GOT AAAALL THE ENDINGS YOU COULD EVER HOPE FOR...
THE REALLY SCARY STUFF
NOT BROKEN JUST TAKING A BREAK
WHERE ARE YOU? C'MON, I'M A LITTLE FREAKED OUT...
THE REALLY SCARY STUFF
SERIOUSLY, WHERE ARE YOU?!
NOT BROKEN JUST TAKING A BREAK

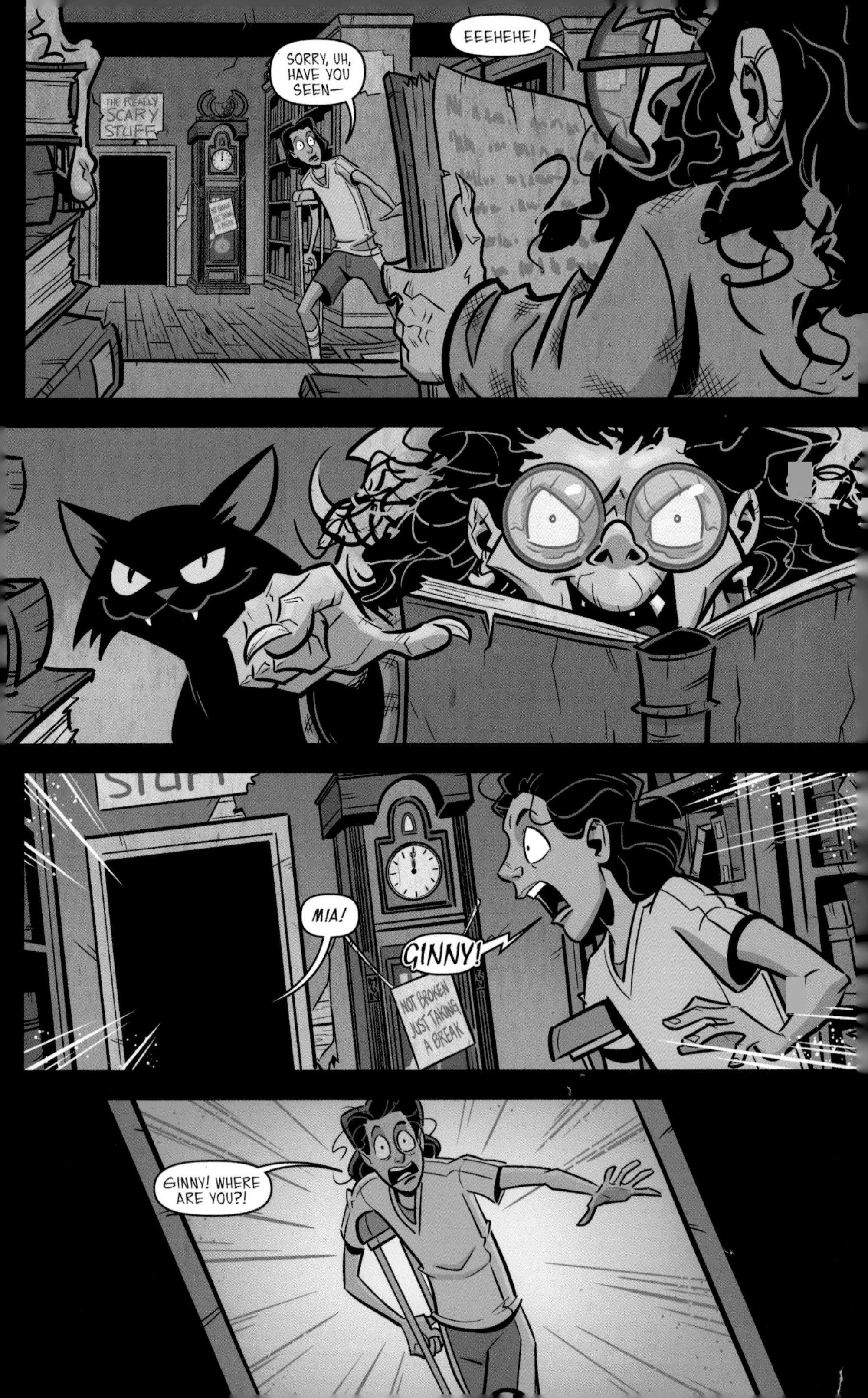
THE REALLY SCARY STUFF
SORRY, UH, HAVE YOU SEEN—
EEEHEHE!
MIA!
GINNY!
NOT BROKEN JUST TAKING A BREAK
GINNY! WHERE ARE YOU?!

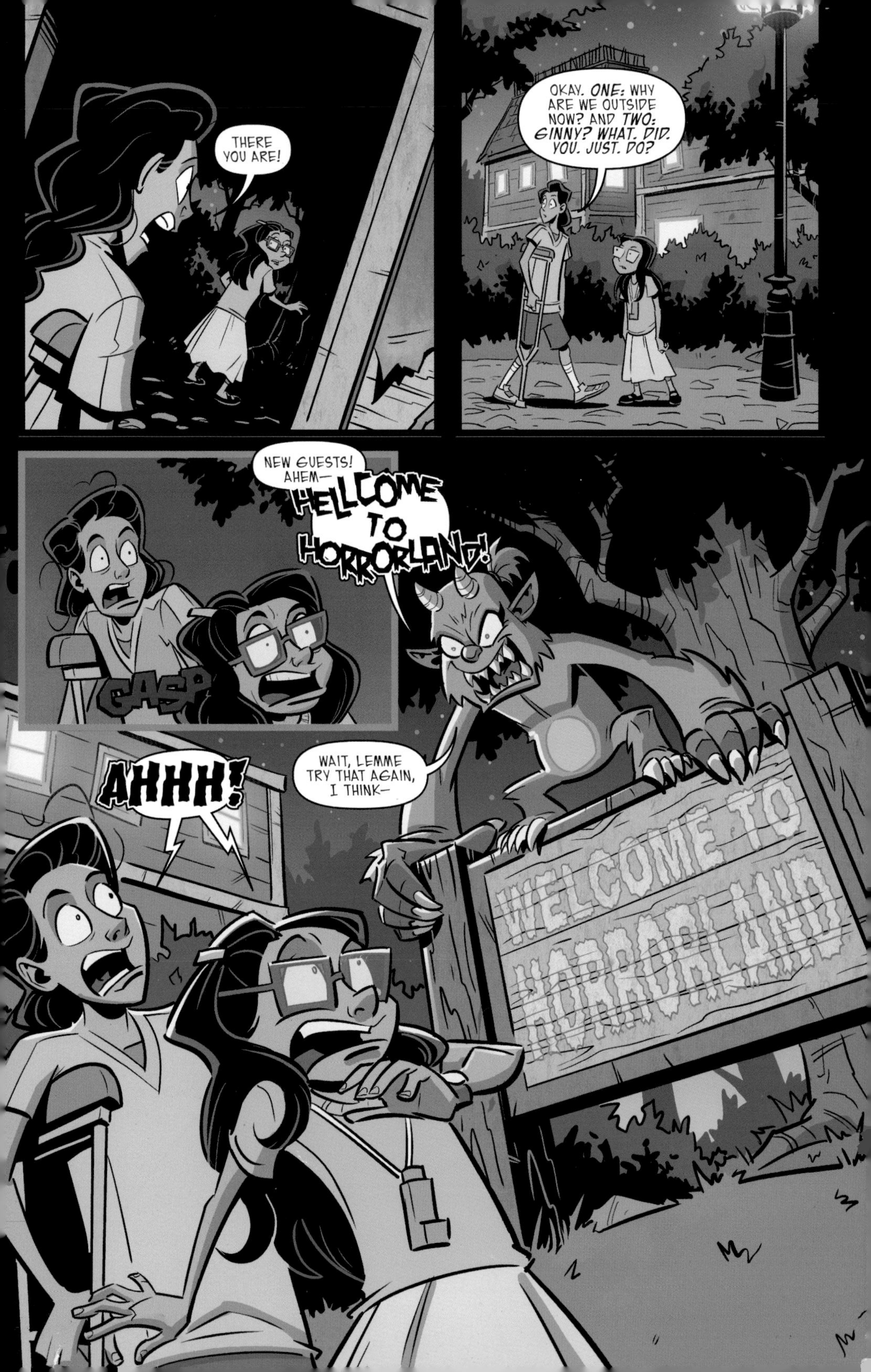
THERE YOU ARE!
OKAY. ONE: WHY ARE WE OUTSIDE NOW? AND TWO: GINNY? WHAT. DID. YOU. JUST. DO?
NEW GUESTS! AHEM—
HELLCOME TO HORRORLAND!
GASP
AHHH!
WAIT, LEMME TRY THAT AGAIN, I THINK—
WELCOME TO HORRORLAND

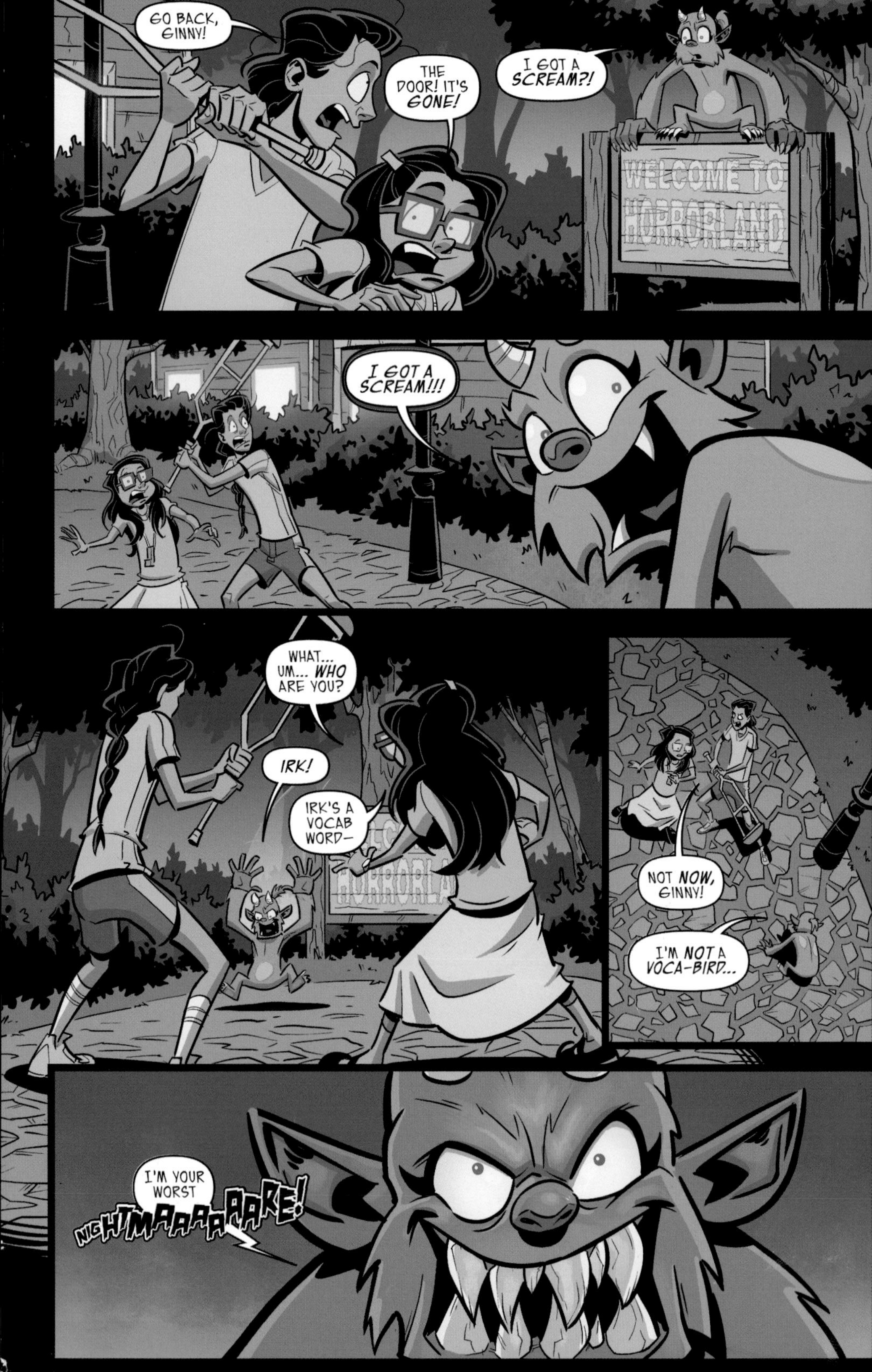
GO BACK, GINNY!
THE DOOR! IT'S GONE!
I GOT A SCREAM?!
WELCOME TO HORRORLAND
I GOT A SCREAM!!!
WHAT... UM... WHO ARE YOU?
IRK!
IRK'S A VOCAB WORD—
NOT NOW, GINNY!
I'M NOT A VOCA-BIRD...
I'M YOUR WORST NIGHTMAAAAAARE!

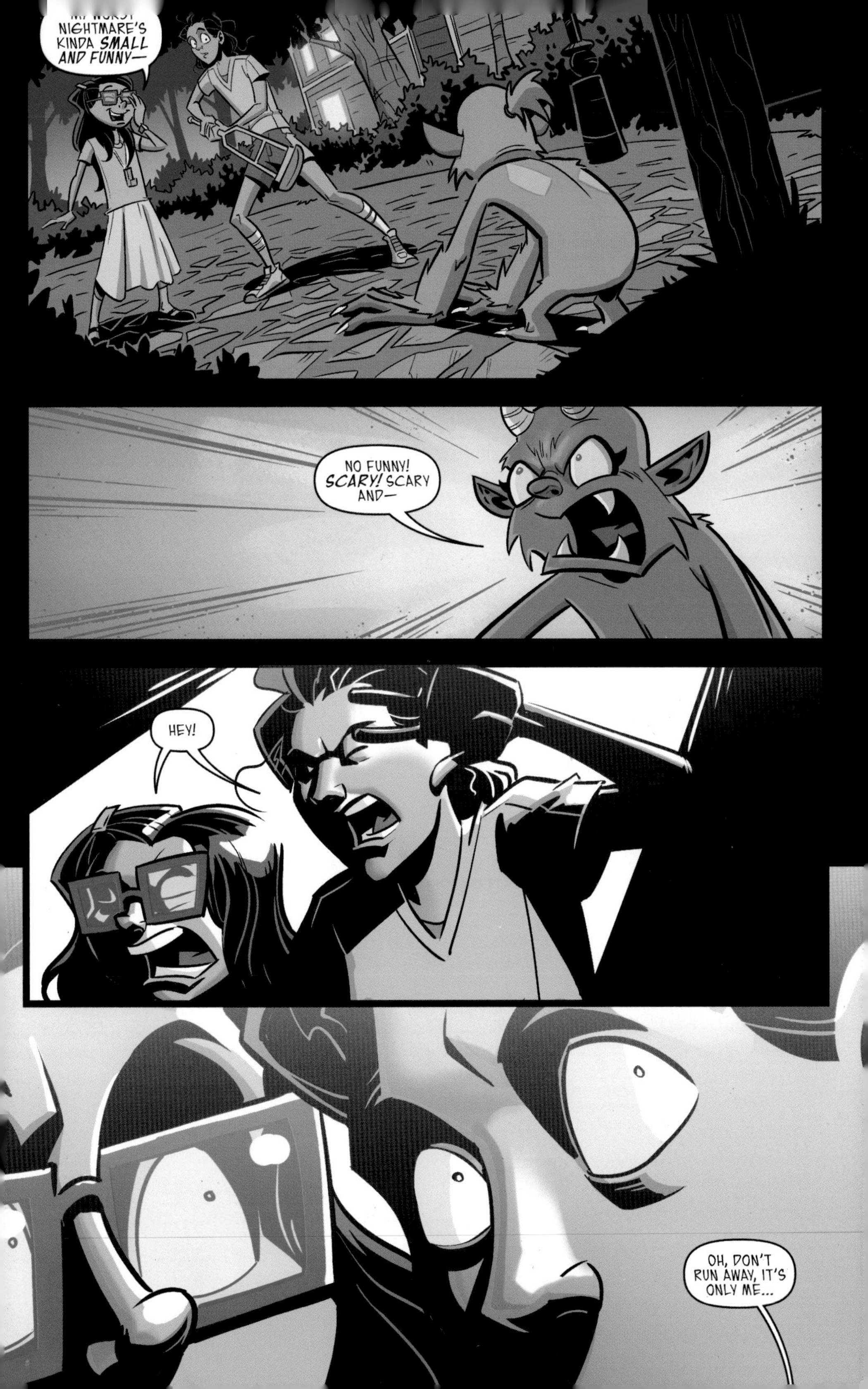

NIGHTMARE'S KINDA **SMALL** AND FUNNY—
NO FUNNY! ***SCARY!*** SCARY AND—
HEY!
OH, DON'T RUN AWAY, IT'S ONLY ME...

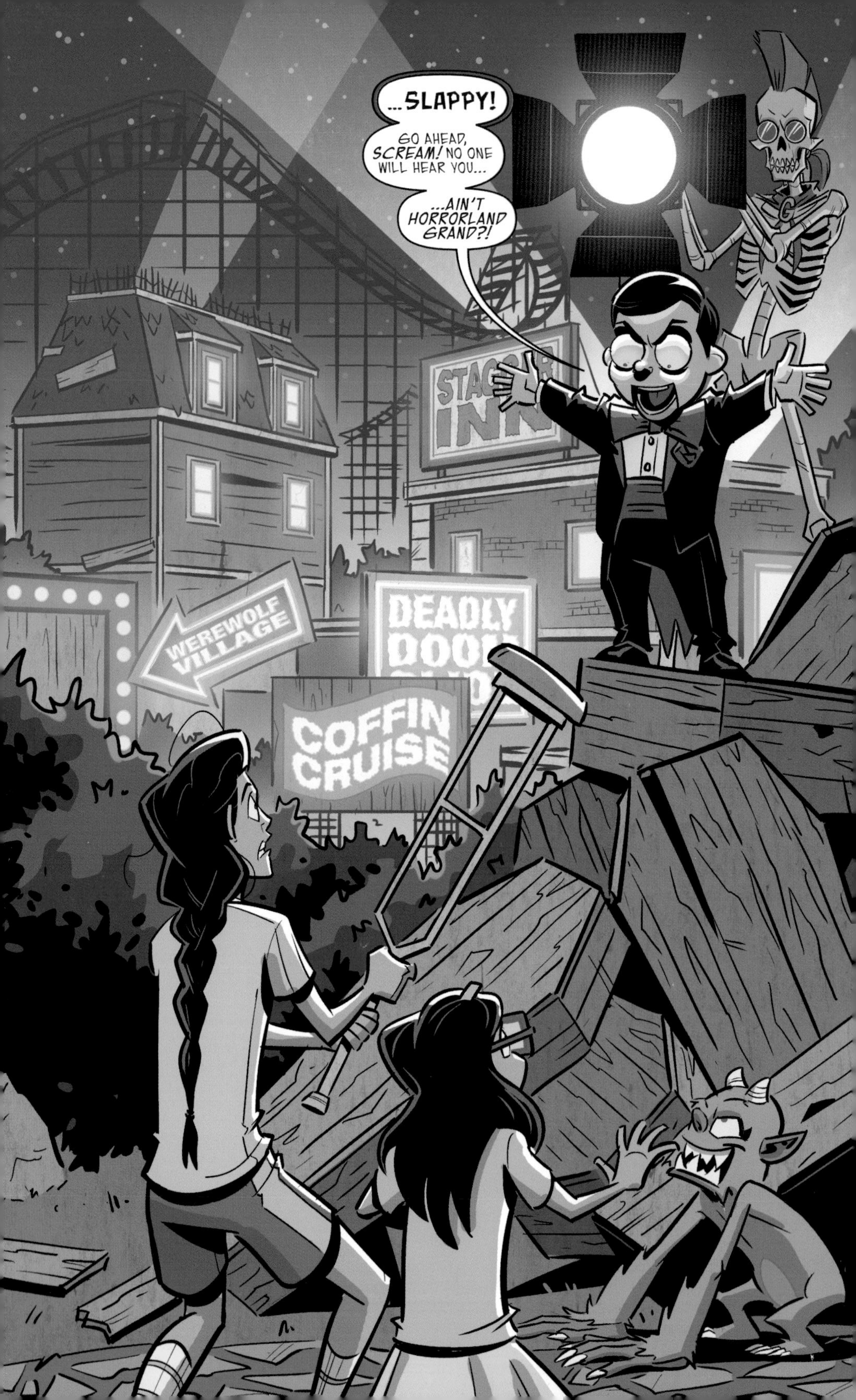
...SLAPPY!
GO AHEAD, SCREAM! NO ONE WILL HEAR YOU...
...AIN'T HORRORLAND GRAND?!
STAGGER INN
WEREWOLF VILLAGE
DEADLY DOOM
COFFIN CRUISE

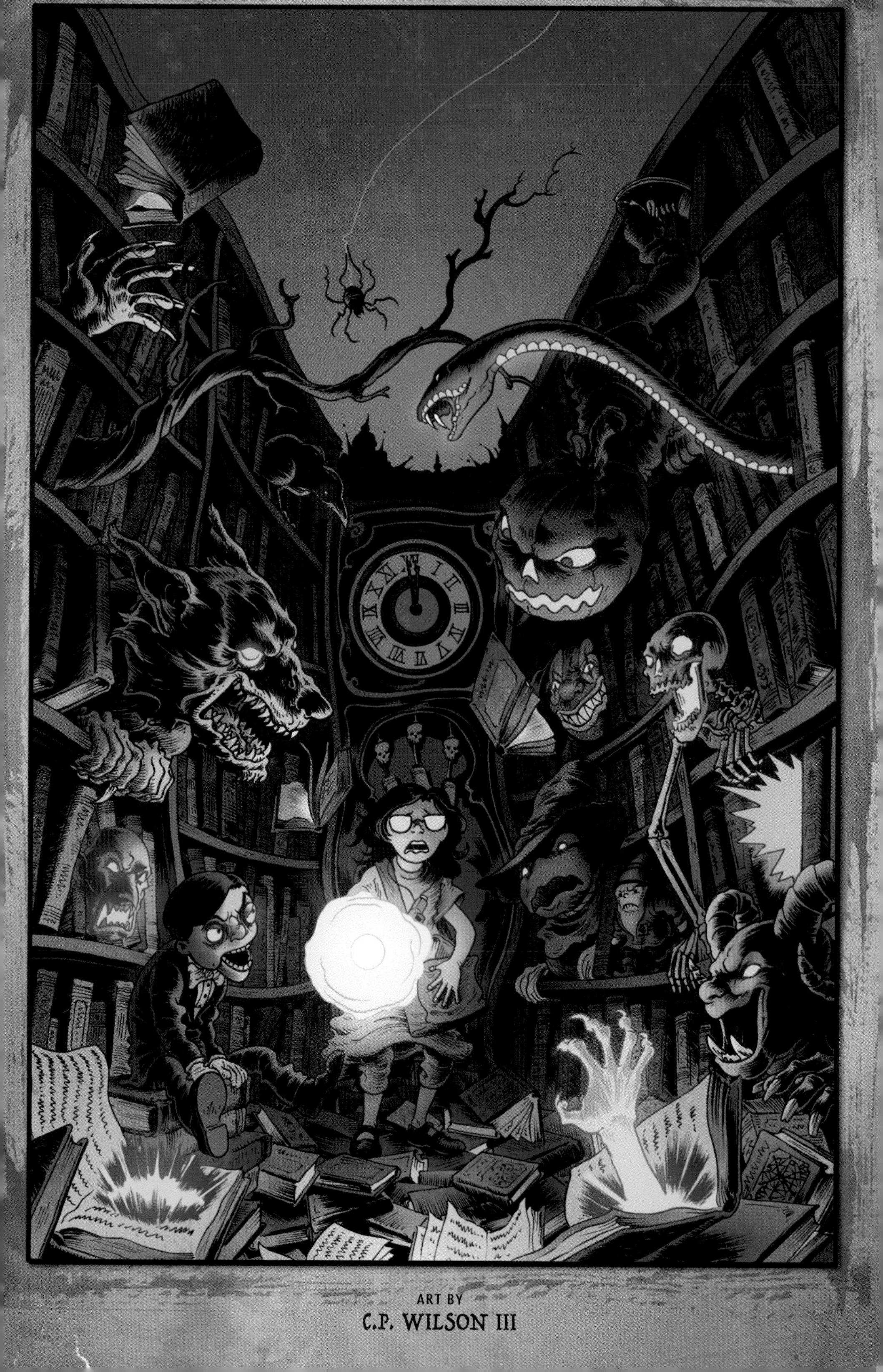

ART BY
C.P. WILSON III

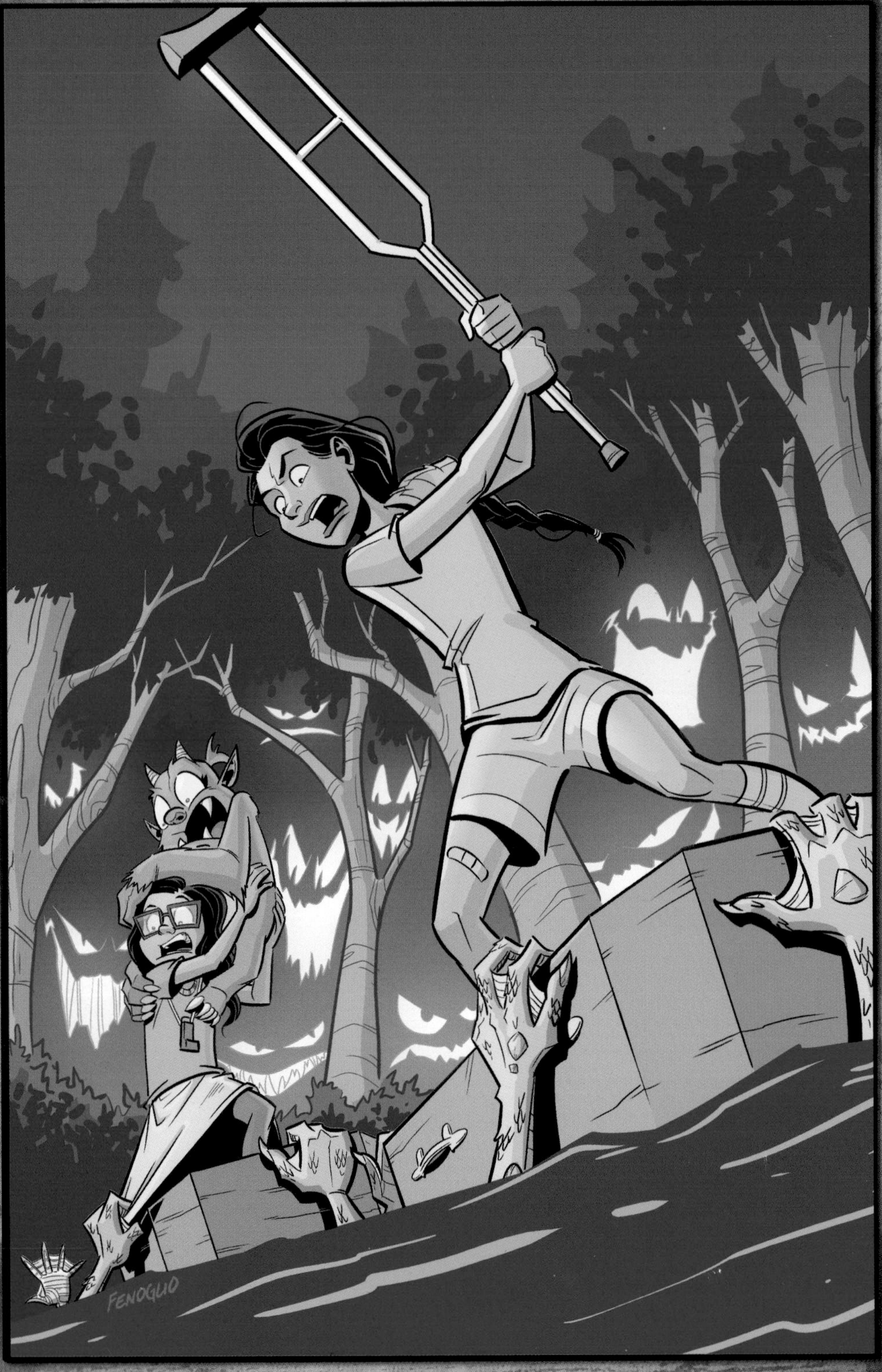
FENOGLIO

ART BY
CHRIS FENOGLIO

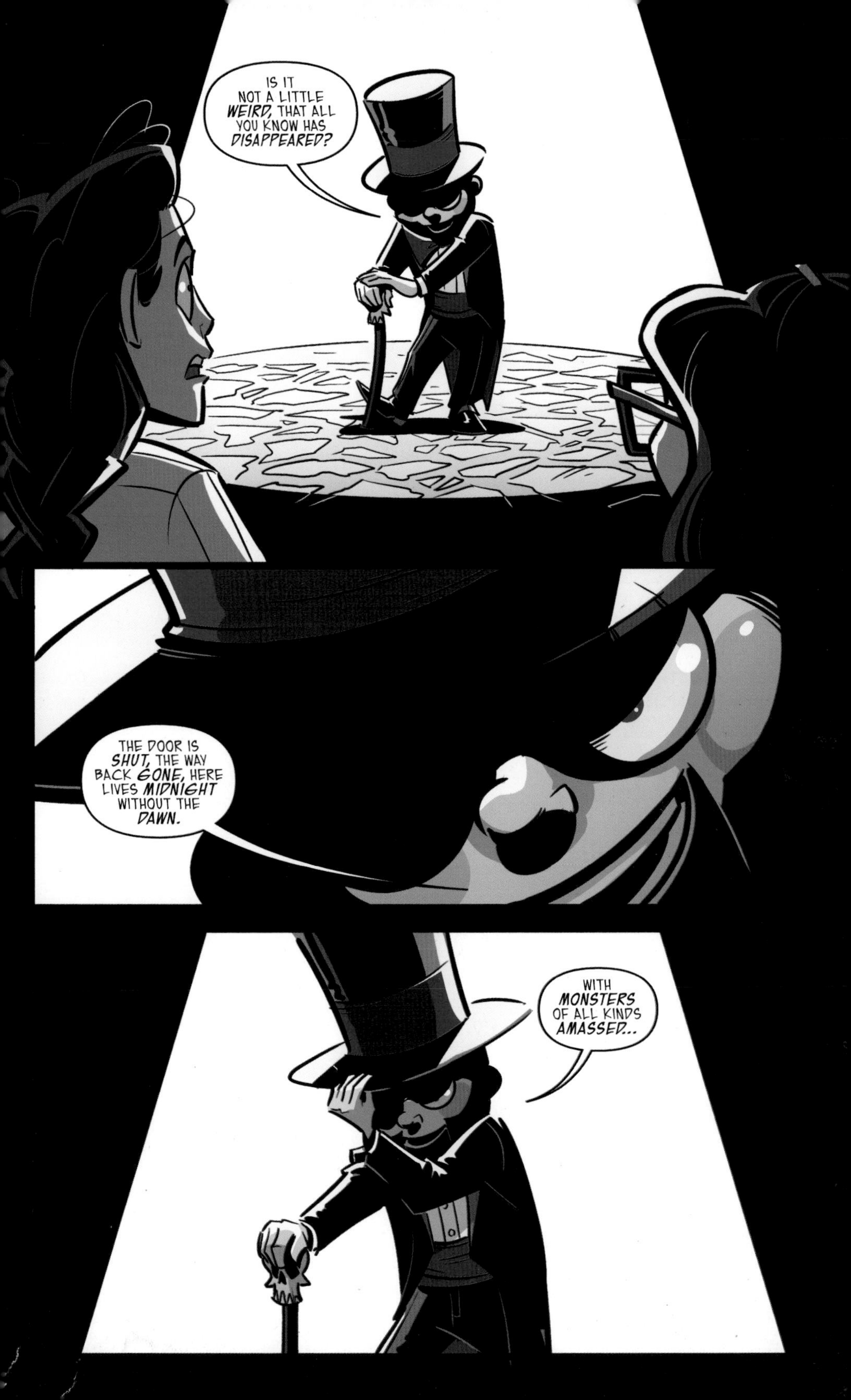
IS IT NOT A LITTLE WEIRD, THAT ALL YOU KNOW HAS DISAPPEARED?
THE DOOR IS SHUT, THE WAY BACK GONE, HERE LIVES MIDNIGHT WITHOUT THE DAWN.
WITH MONSTERS OF ALL KINDS AMASSED...

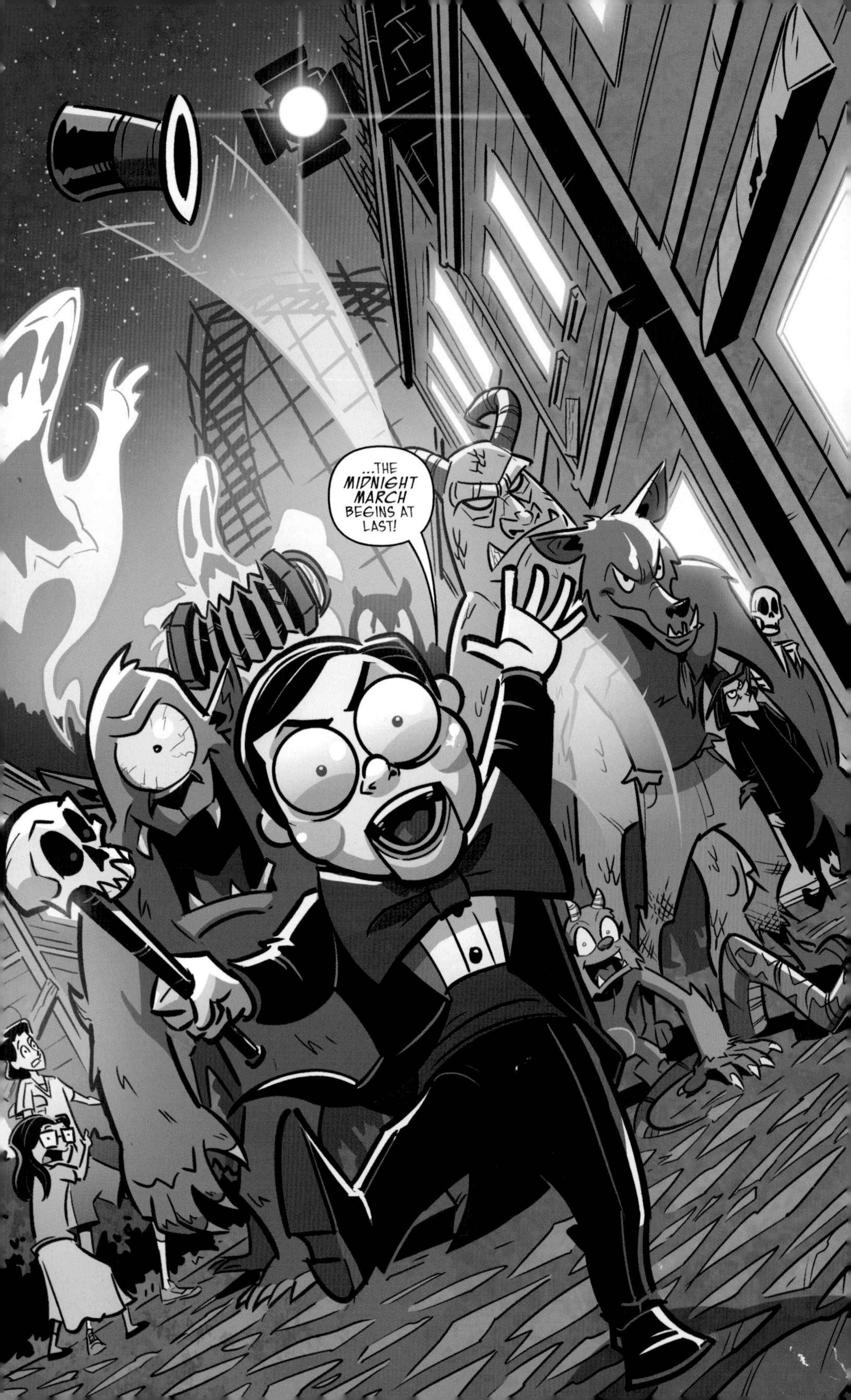
...THE MIDNIGHT MARCH BEGINS AT LAST!

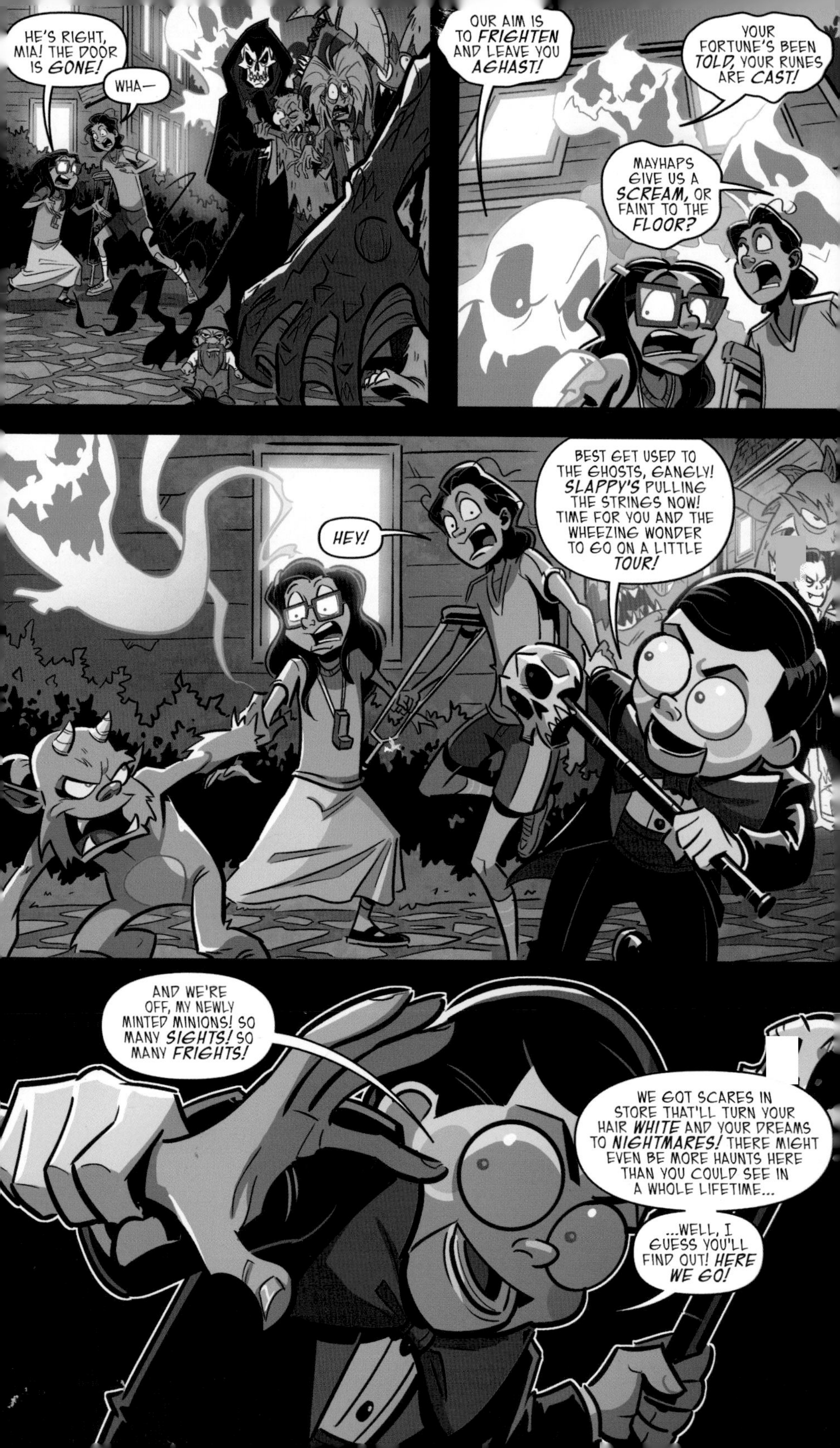
HE'S RIGHT, MIA! THE DOOR IS GONE!
WHA—
OUR AIM IS TO FRIGHTEN AND LEAVE YOU AGHAST!
YOUR FORTUNE'S BEEN TOLD, YOUR RUNES ARE CAST!
MAYHAPS GIVE US A SCREAM, OR FAINT TO THE FLOOR?
HEY!
BEST GET USED TO THE GHOSTS, GANGLY! SLAPPY'S PULLING THE STRINGS NOW! TIME FOR YOU AND THE WHEEZING WONDER TO GO ON A LITTLE TOUR!
AND WE'RE OFF, MY NEWLY MINTED MINIONS! SO MANY SIGHTS! SO MANY FRIGHTS!
WE GOT SCARES IN STORE THAT'LL TURN YOUR HAIR WHITE AND YOUR DREAMS TO NIGHTMARES! THERE MIGHT EVEN BE MORE HAUNTS HERE THAN YOU COULD SEE IN A WHOLE LIFETIME...
...WELL, I GUESS YOU'LL FIND OUT! HERE WE GO!

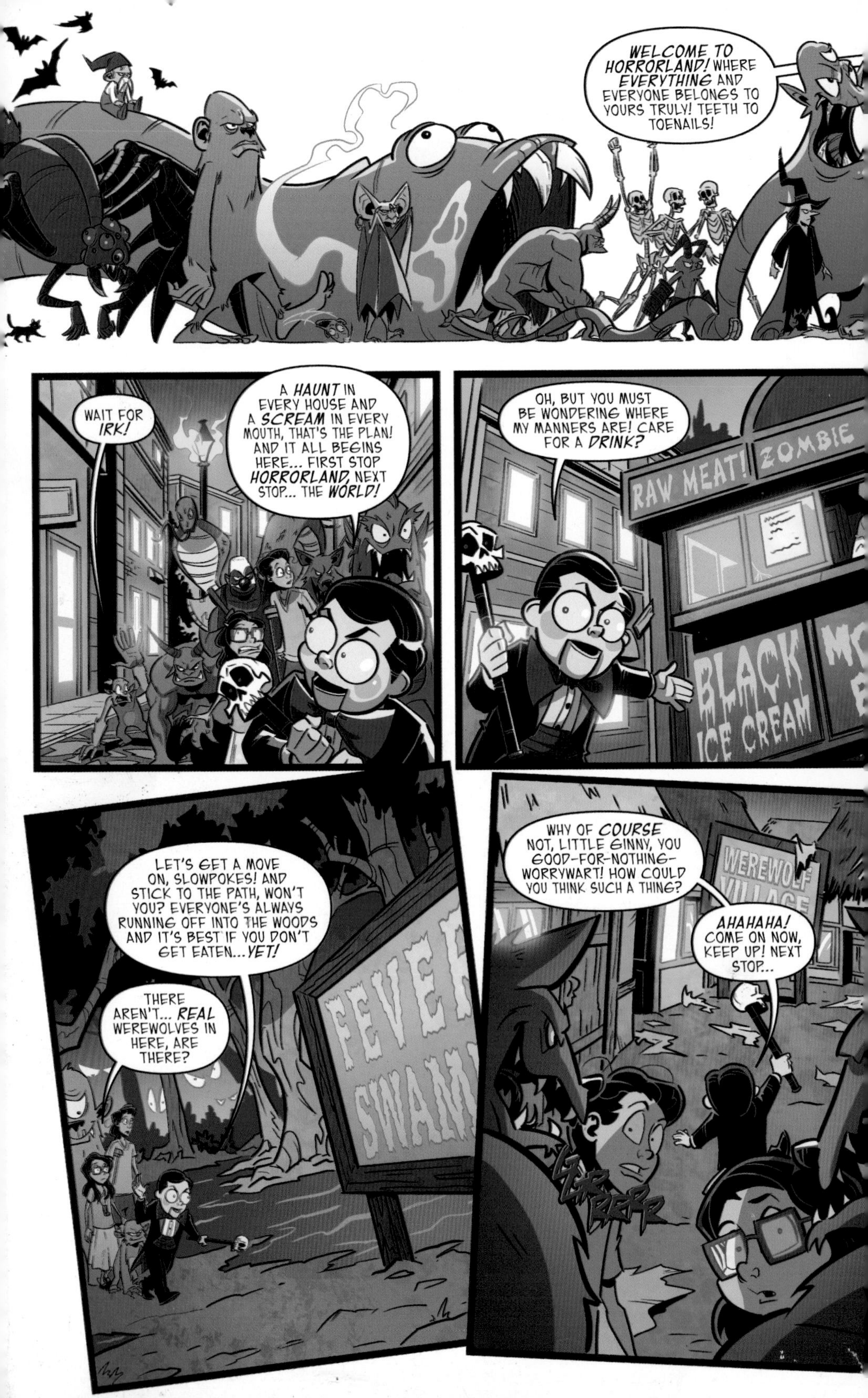
WELCOME TO HORRORLAND! WHERE EVERYTHING AND EVERYONE BELONGS TO YOURS TRULY! TEETH TO TOENAILS!
WAIT FOR IRK!
A HAUNT IN EVERY HOUSE AND A SCREAM IN EVERY MOUTH, THAT'S THE PLAN! AND IT ALL BEGINS HERE... FIRST STOP HORRORLAND, NEXT STOP... THE WORLD!
OH, BUT YOU MUST BE WONDERING WHERE MY MANNERS ARE! CARE FOR A DRINK?
RAW MEAT!
ZOMBIE
BLACK ICE CREAM
LET'S GET A MOVE ON, SLOWPOKES! AND STICK TO THE PATH, WON'T YOU? EVERYONE'S ALWAYS RUNNING OFF INTO THE WOODS AND IT'S BEST IF YOU DON'T GET EATEN...YET!
THERE AREN'T... REAL WEREWOLVES IN HERE, ARE THERE?
WHY OF COURSE NOT, LITTLE GINNY, YOU GOOD-FOR-NOTHING-WORRYWART! HOW COULD YOU THINK SUCH A THING?
WEREWOLF
AHAHAHA! COME ON NOW, KEEP UP! NEXT STOP...

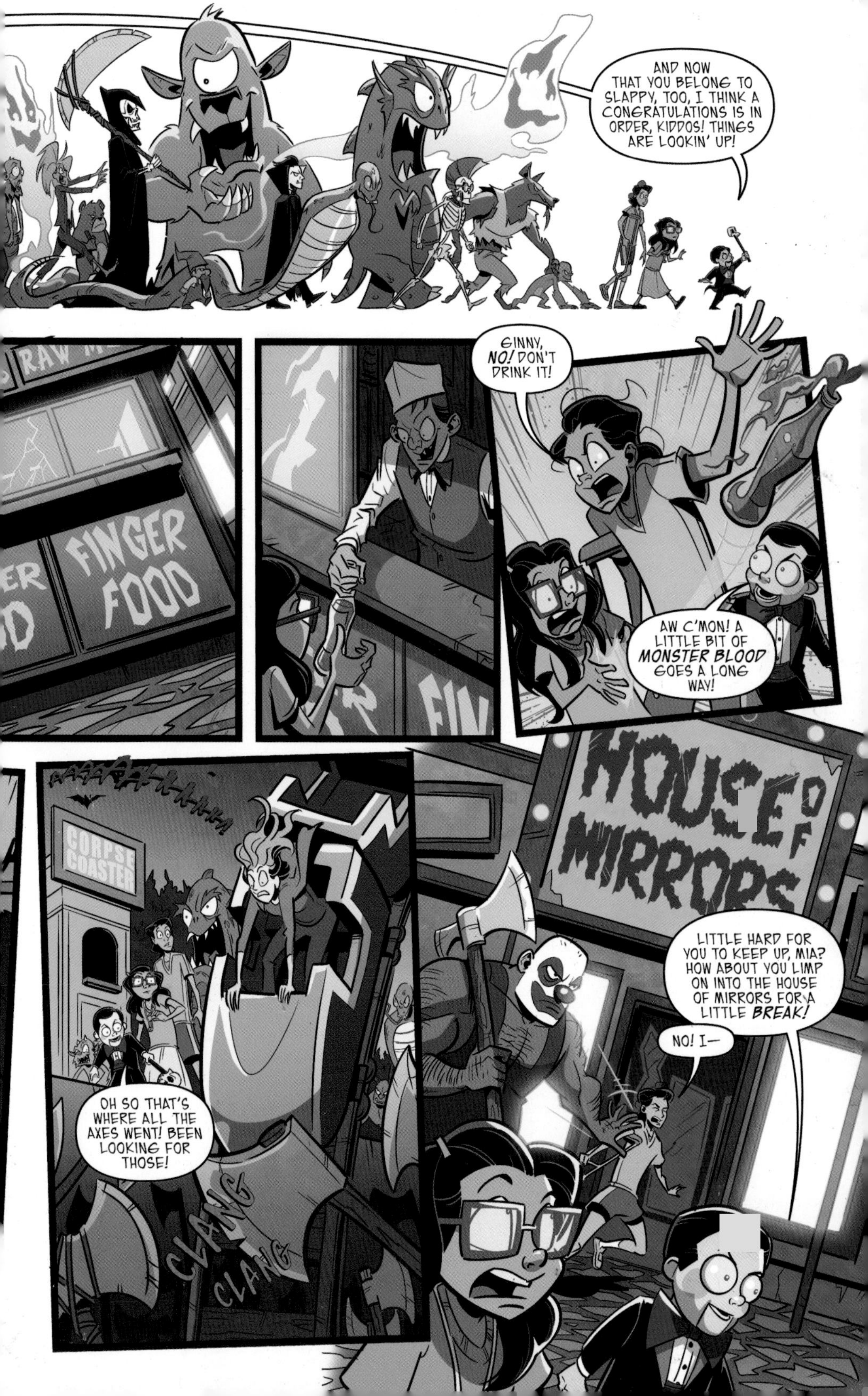
AND NOW THAT YOU BELONG TO SLAPPY, TOO, I THINK A CONGRATULATIONS IS IN ORDER, KIDDOS! THINGS ARE LOOKIN' UP!
FINGER FOOD
GINNY, NO! DON'T DRINK IT!
AW C'MON! A LITTLE BIT OF MONSTER BLOOD GOES A LONG WAY!
CORPSE COASTER
HOUSE OF MIRRORS
OH SO THAT'S WHERE ALL THE AXES WENT! BEEN LOOKING FOR THOSE!
CLANG
CLANG
LITTLE HARD FOR YOU TO KEEP UP, MIA? HOW ABOUT YOU LIMP ON INTO THE HOUSE OF MIRRORS FOR A LITTLE BREAK!
NO! I—

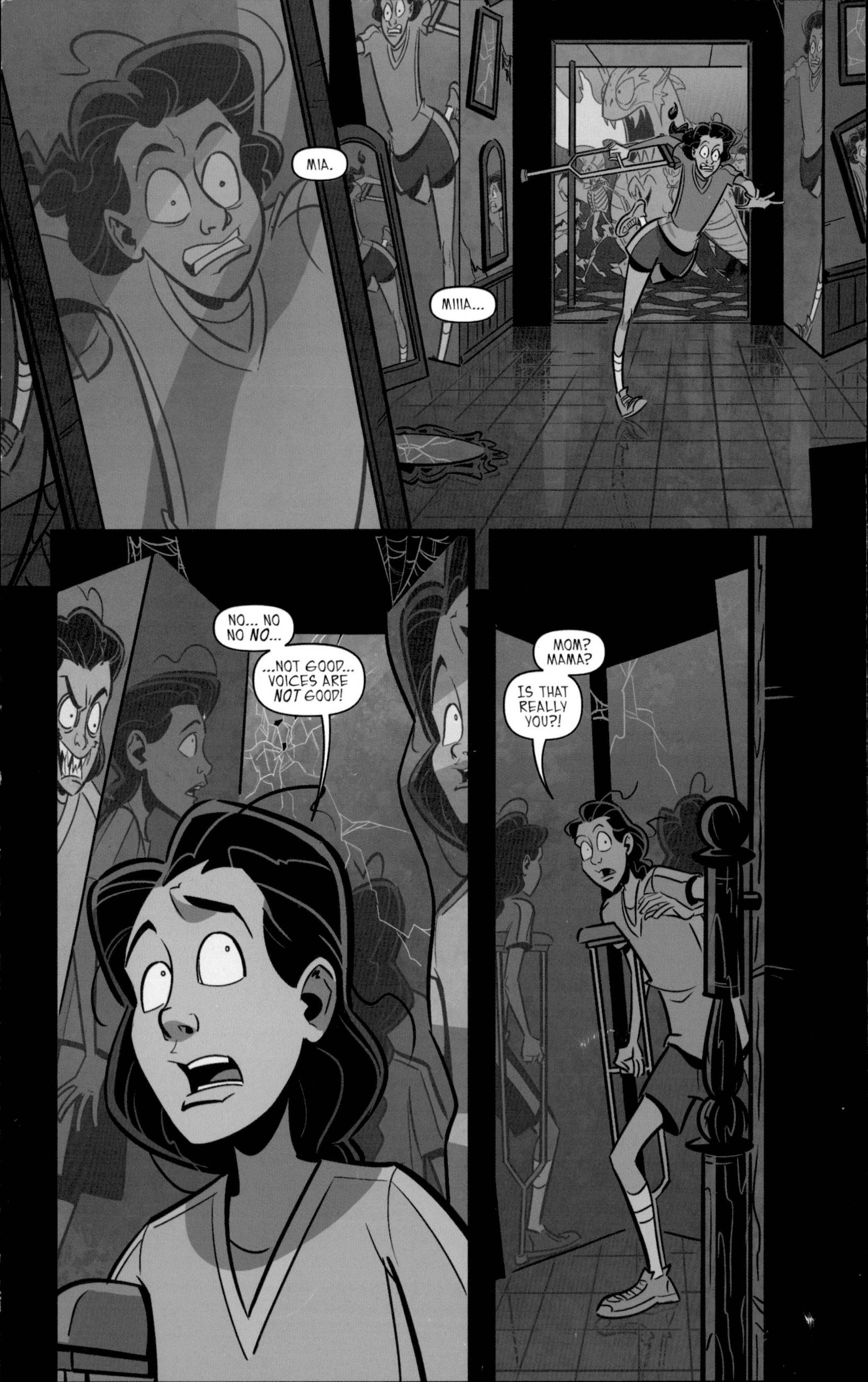
MIA.
MIIIA...
NO... NO NO NO...
...NOT GOOD... VOICES ARE NOT GOOD!
MOM? MAMA?
IS THAT REALLY YOU?!

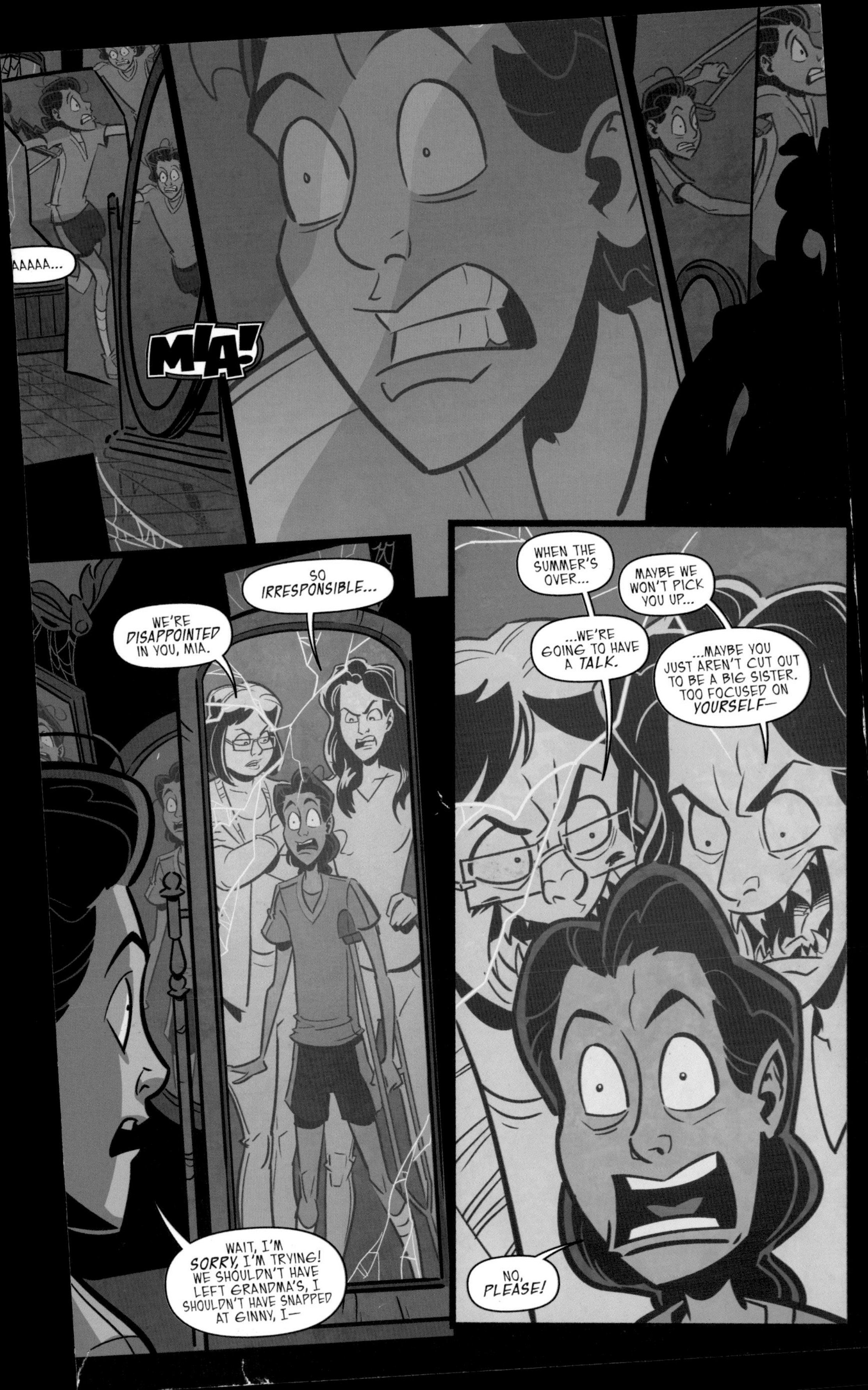
AAAAA...
MIA!
SO IRRESPONSIBLE...
WE'RE DISAPPOINTED IN YOU, MIA.
WAIT, I'M SORRY, I'M TRYING! WE SHOULDN'T HAVE LEFT GRANDMA'S, I SHOULDN'T HAVE SNAPPED AT GINNY, I—
WHEN THE SUMMER'S OVER...
...WE'RE GOING TO HAVE A TALK.
MAYBE WE WON'T PICK YOU UP...
...MAYBE YOU JUST AREN'T CUT OUT TO BE A BIG SISTER. TOO FOCUSED ON YOURSELF—
NO, PLEASE!

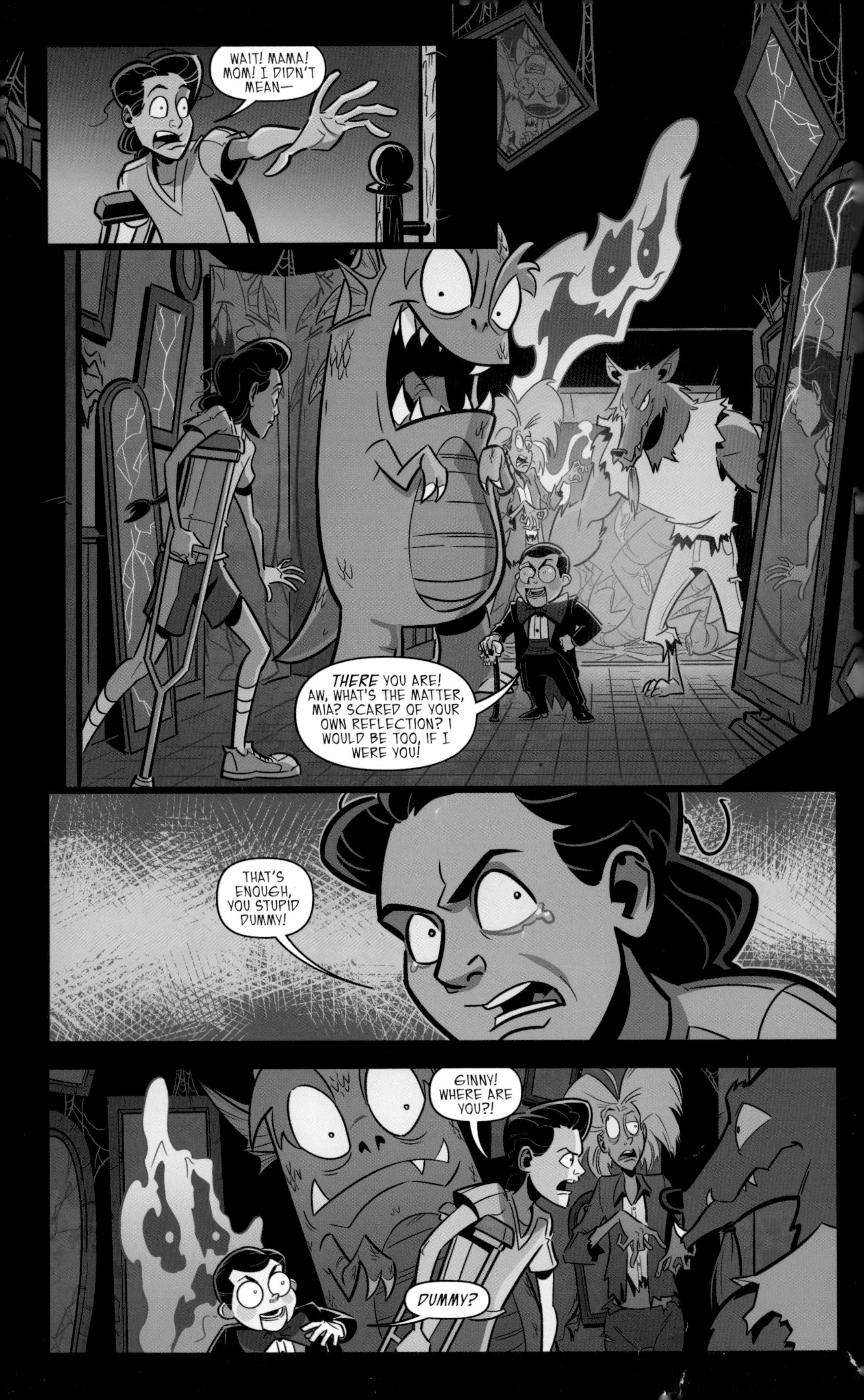
WAIT! MAMA! MOM! I DIDN'T MEAN—
THERE YOU ARE! AW, WHAT'S THE MATTER, MIA? SCARED OF YOUR OWN REFLECTION? I WOULD BE TOO, IF I WERE YOU!
THAT'S ENOUGH, YOU STUPID DUMMY!
GINNY! WHERE ARE YOU?!
DUMMY?

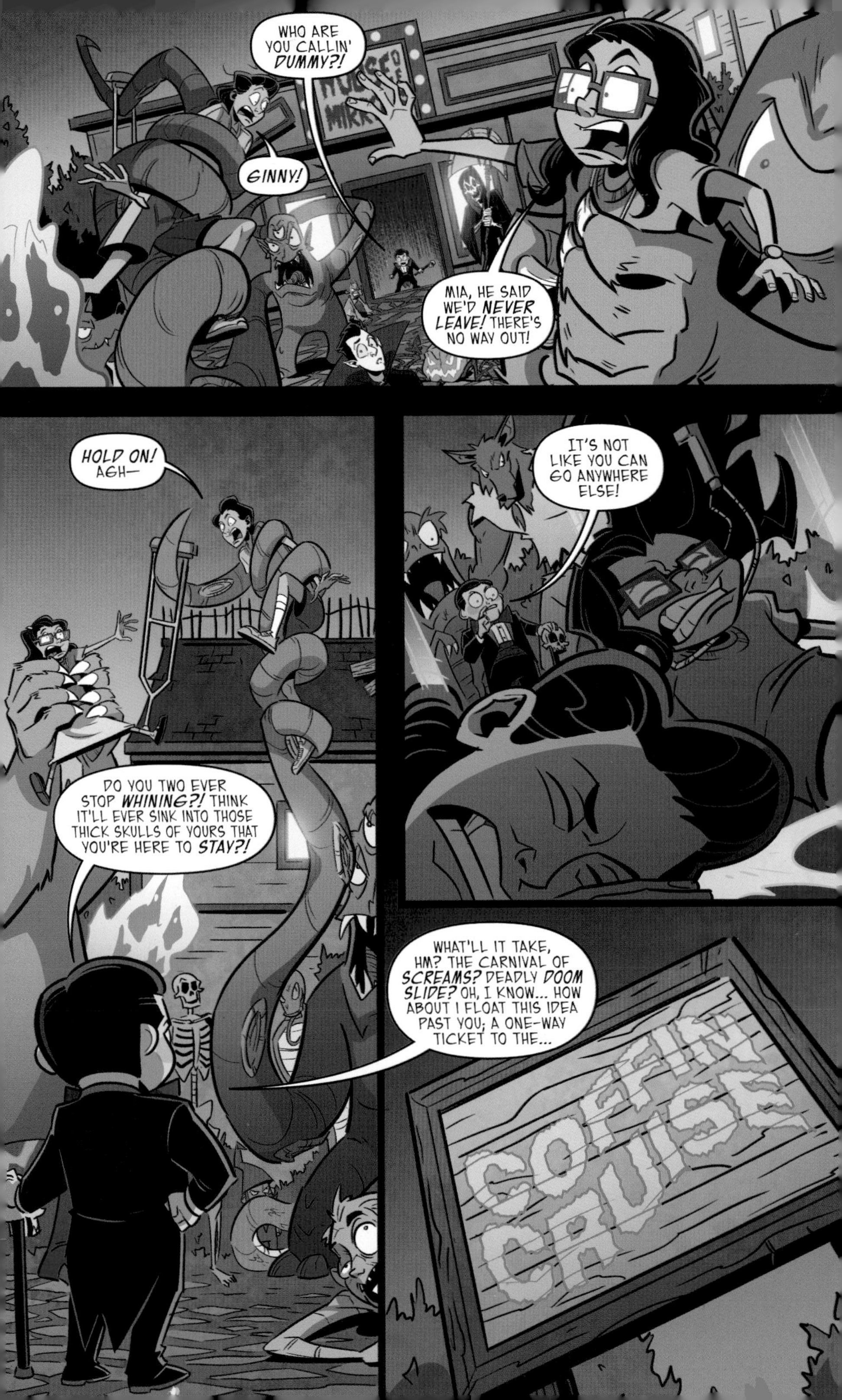
WHO ARE YOU CALLIN' DUMMY?!
GINNY!
MIA, HE SAID WE'D NEVER LEAVE! THERE'S NO WAY OUT!
HOLD ON! AGH—
IT'S NOT LIKE YOU CAN GO ANYWHERE ELSE!
DO YOU TWO EVER STOP WHINING?! THINK IT'LL EVER SINK INTO THOSE THICK SKULLS OF YOURS THAT YOU'RE HERE TO STAY?!
WHAT'LL IT TAKE, HM? THE CARNIVAL OF SCREAMS? DEADLY DOOM SLIDE? OH, I KNOW... HOW ABOUT I FLOAT THIS IDEA PAST YOU; A ONE-WAY TICKET TO THE...
COFFIN CRUISE

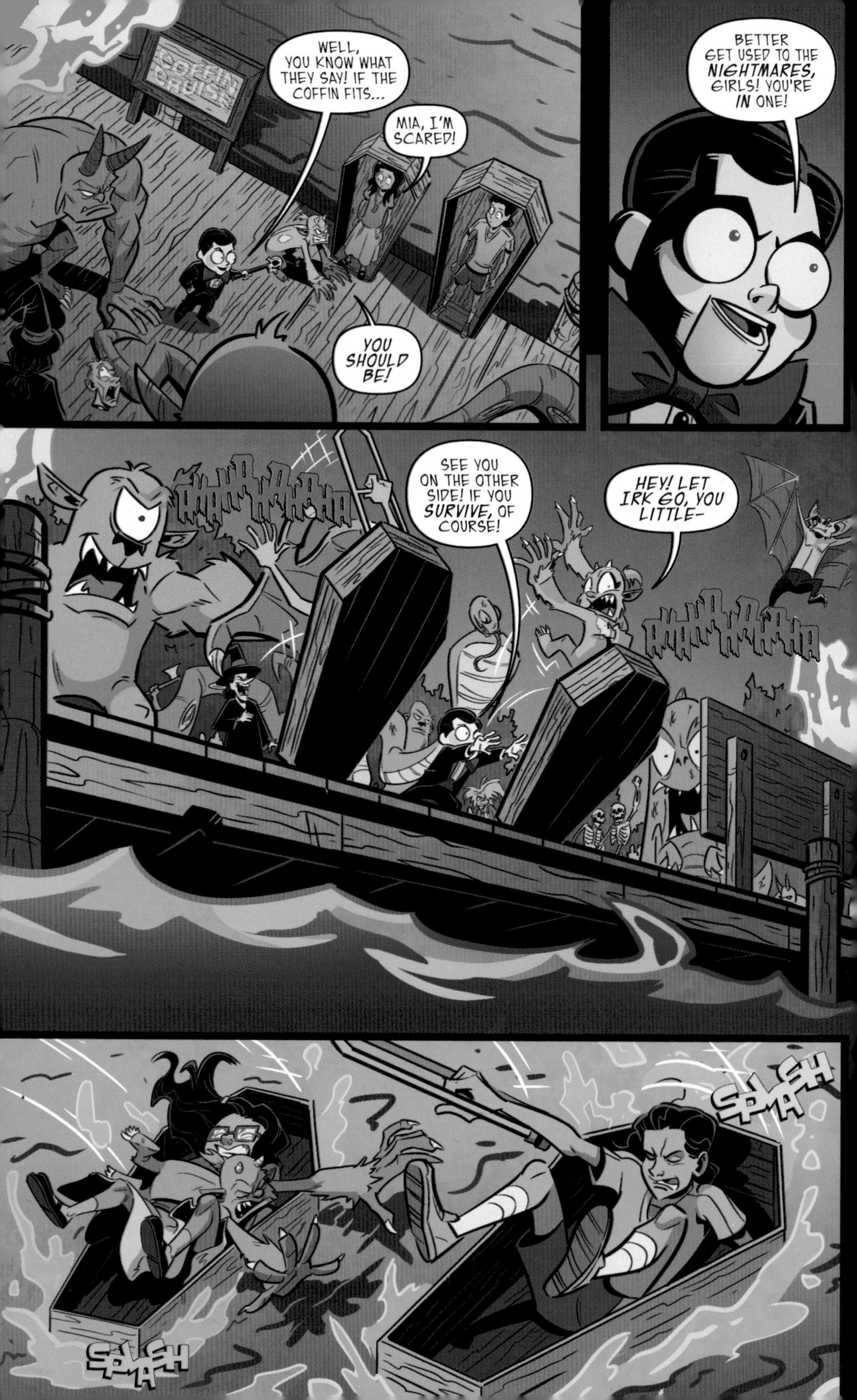
COFFIN CRUISE
WELL, YOU KNOW WHAT THEY SAY! IF THE COFFIN FITS...
MIA, I'M SCARED!
YOU SHOULD BE!
BETTER GET USED TO THE NIGHTMARES, GIRLS! YOU'RE IN ONE!
AHHAHAHAHA
SEE YOU ON THE OTHER SIDE! IF YOU SURVIVE, OF COURSE!
HEY! LET IRK GO, YOU LITTLE-
AHHAHAHAHA
SPLASH
SPLASH

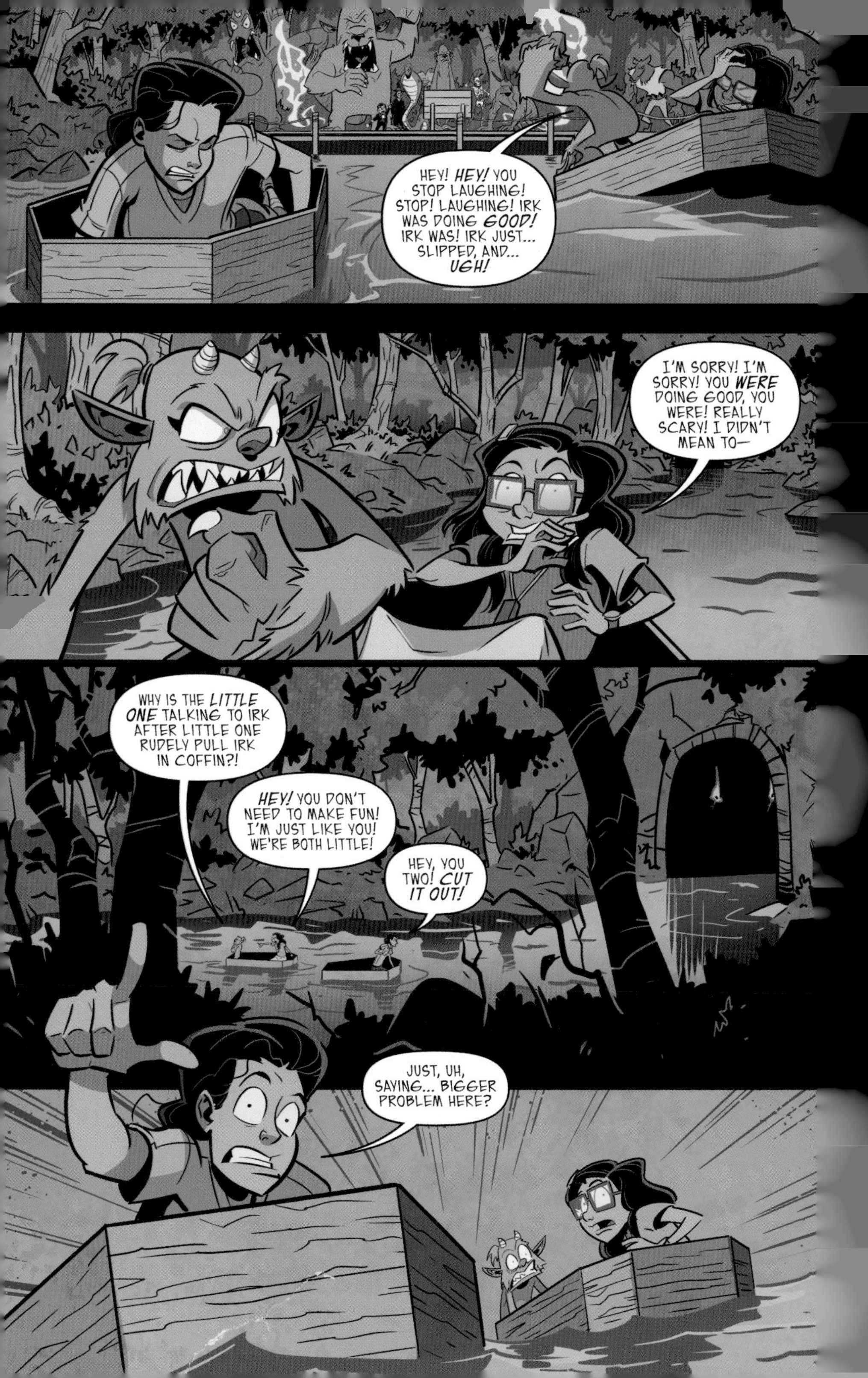
HEY! HEY! YOU STOP LAUGHING! STOP! LAUGHING! IRK WAS DOING GOOD! IRK WAS! IRK JUST... SLIPPED, AND... UGH!
I'M SORRY! I'M SORRY! YOU WERE DOING GOOD, YOU WERE! REALLY SCARY! I DIDN'T MEAN TO—
WHY IS THE LITTLE ONE TALKING TO IRK AFTER LITTLE ONE RUDELY PULL IRK IN COFFIN?!
HEY! YOU DON'T NEED TO MAKE FUN! I'M JUST LIKE YOU! WE'RE BOTH LITTLE!
HEY, YOU TWO! CUT IT OUT!
JUST, UH, SAYING... BIGGER PROBLEM HERE?

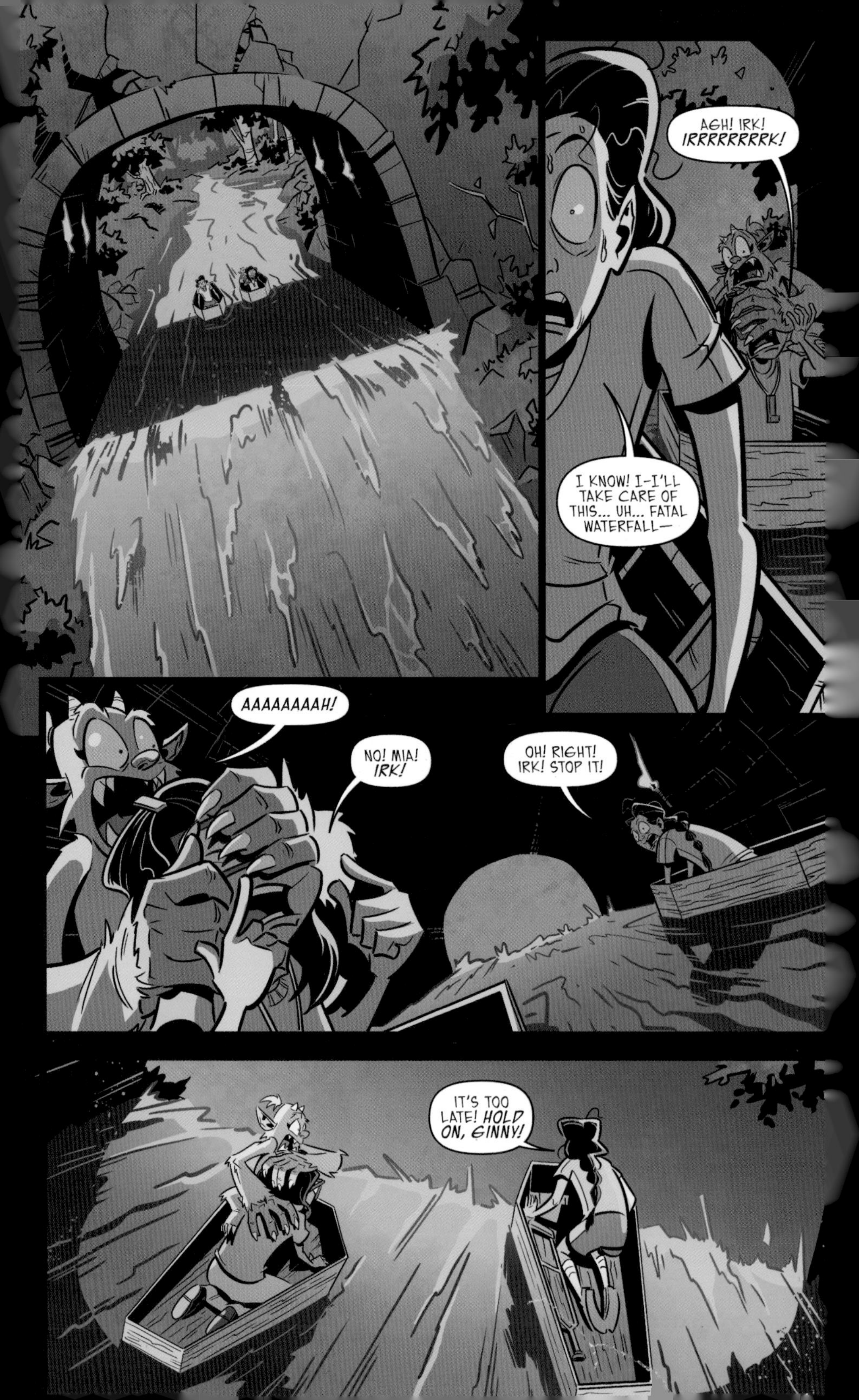
AGH! IRK! IRRRRRRRK!
I KNOW! I-I'LL TAKE CARE OF THIS... UH... FATAL WATERFALL—
AAAAAAAAH!
NO! MIA! IRK!
OH! RIGHT! IRK! STOP IT!
IT'S TOO LATE! HOLD ON, GINNY!

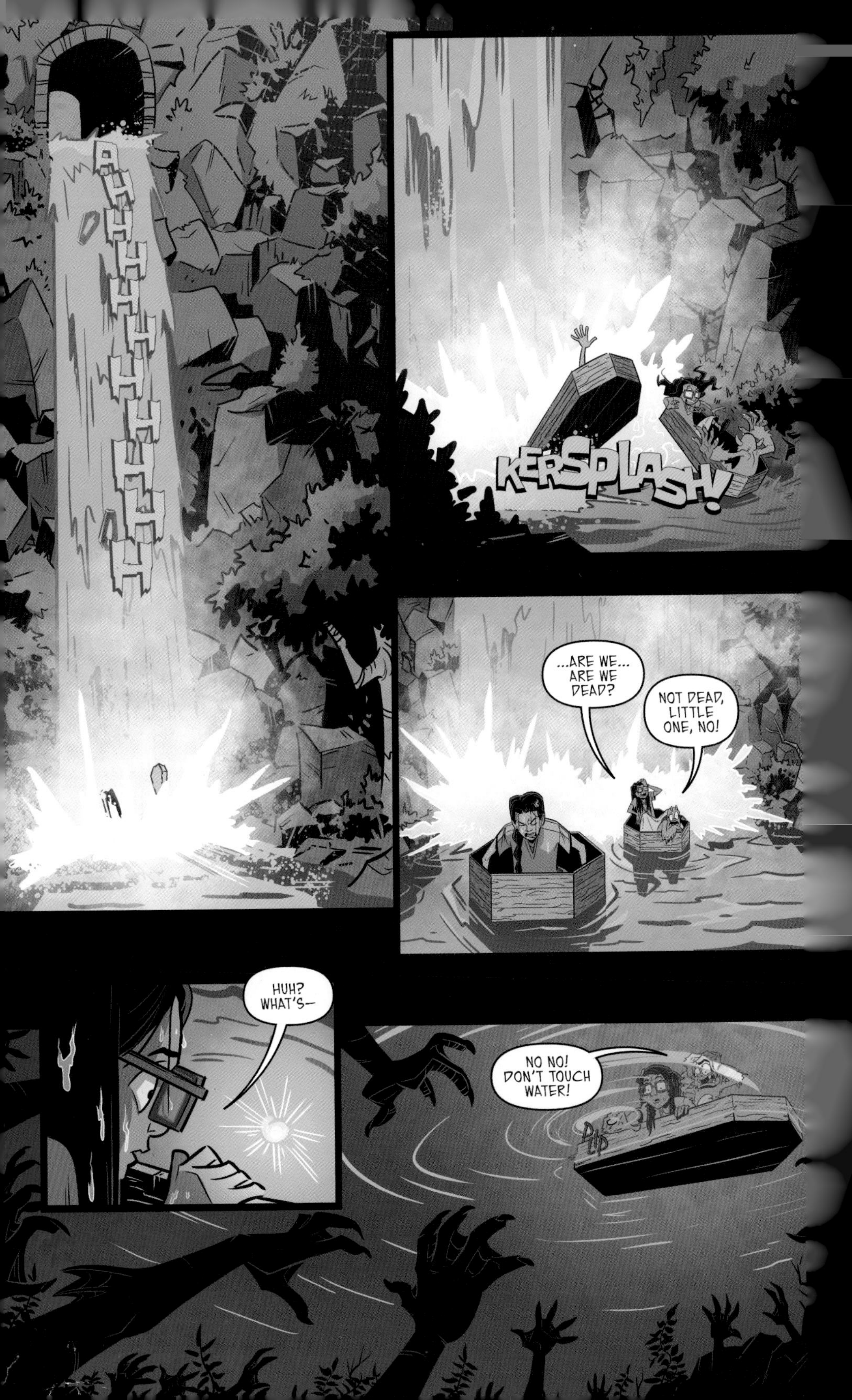
AHHHHHHHHHH
KERSPLASH!
...ARE WE... ARE WE DEAD?
NOT DEAD, LITTLE ONE, NO!
HUH? WHAT'S—
NO NO! DON'T TOUCH WATER!
PLIP

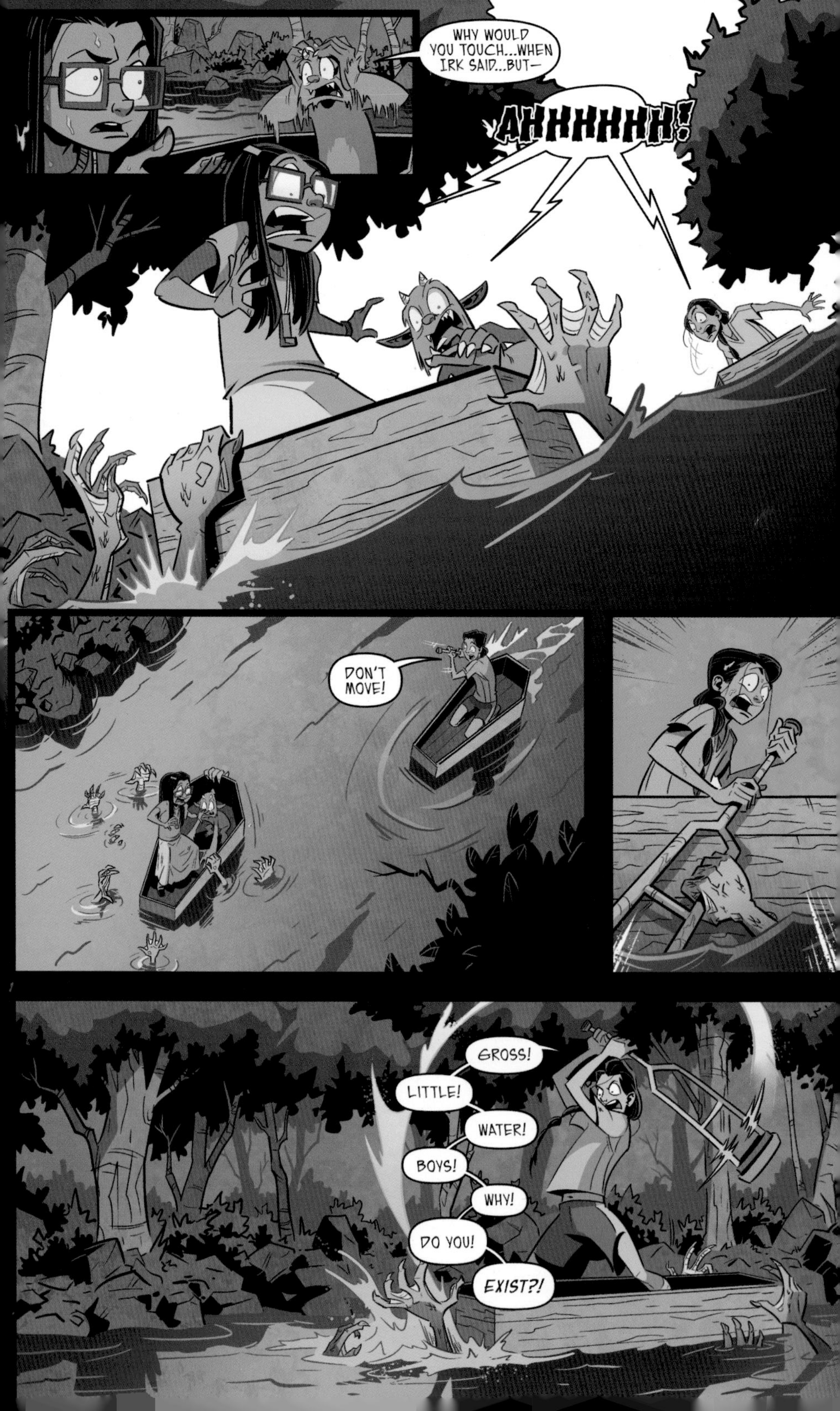
WHY WOULD YOU TOUCH...WHEN IRK SAID...BUT—
AHHHHHHH!
DON'T MOVE!
GROSS!
LITTLE!
WATER!
BOYS!
WHY!
DO YOU!
EXIST?!

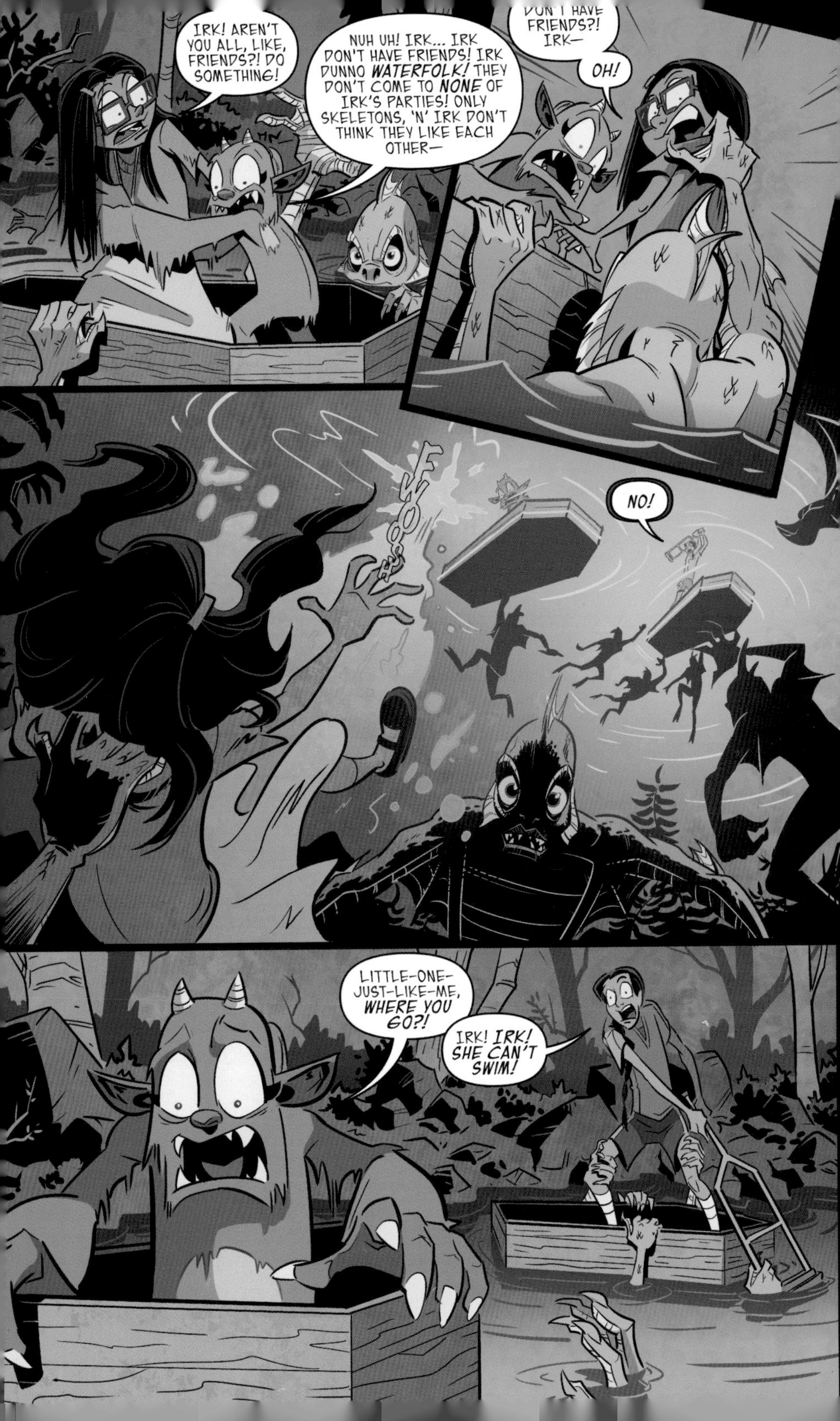
IRK! AREN'T YOU ALL, LIKE, FRIENDS?! DO SOMETHING!
NUH UH! IRK... IRK DON'T HAVE FRIENDS! IRK DUNNO WATERFOLK! THEY DON'T COME TO NONE OF IRK'S PARTIES! ONLY SKELETONS, 'N' IRK DON'T THINK THEY LIKE EACH OTHER—
DON'T HAVE FRIENDS?! IRK—
OH!
FWOOSH
NO!
LITTLE-ONE-JUST-LIKE-ME, WHERE YOU GO?!
IRK! IRK! SHE CAN'T SWIM!

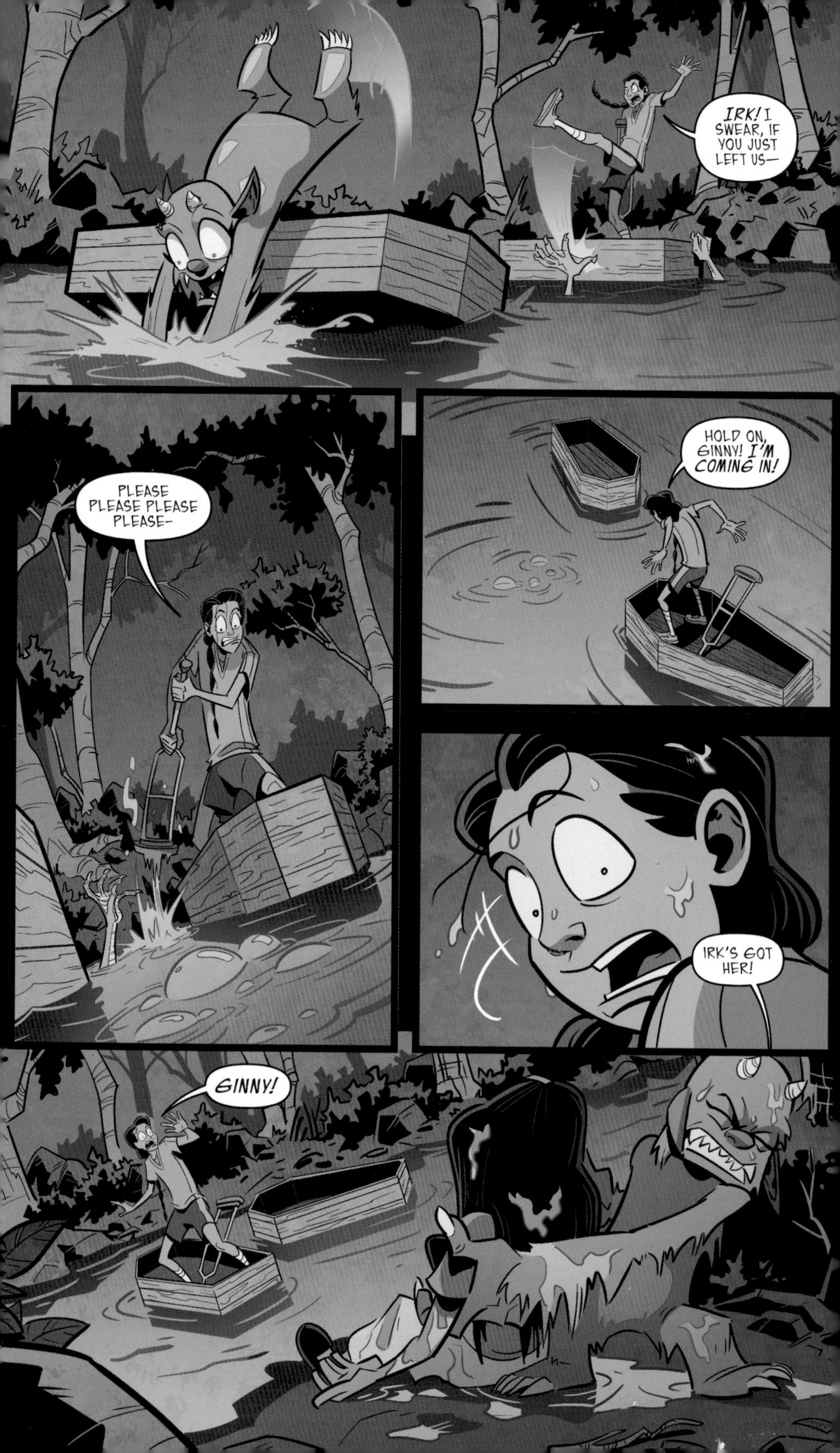
IRK! I SWEAR, IF YOU JUST LEFT US—
PLEASE PLEASE PLEASE PLEASE–
HOLD ON, GINNY! I'M COMING IN!
IRK'S GOT HER!
GINNY!

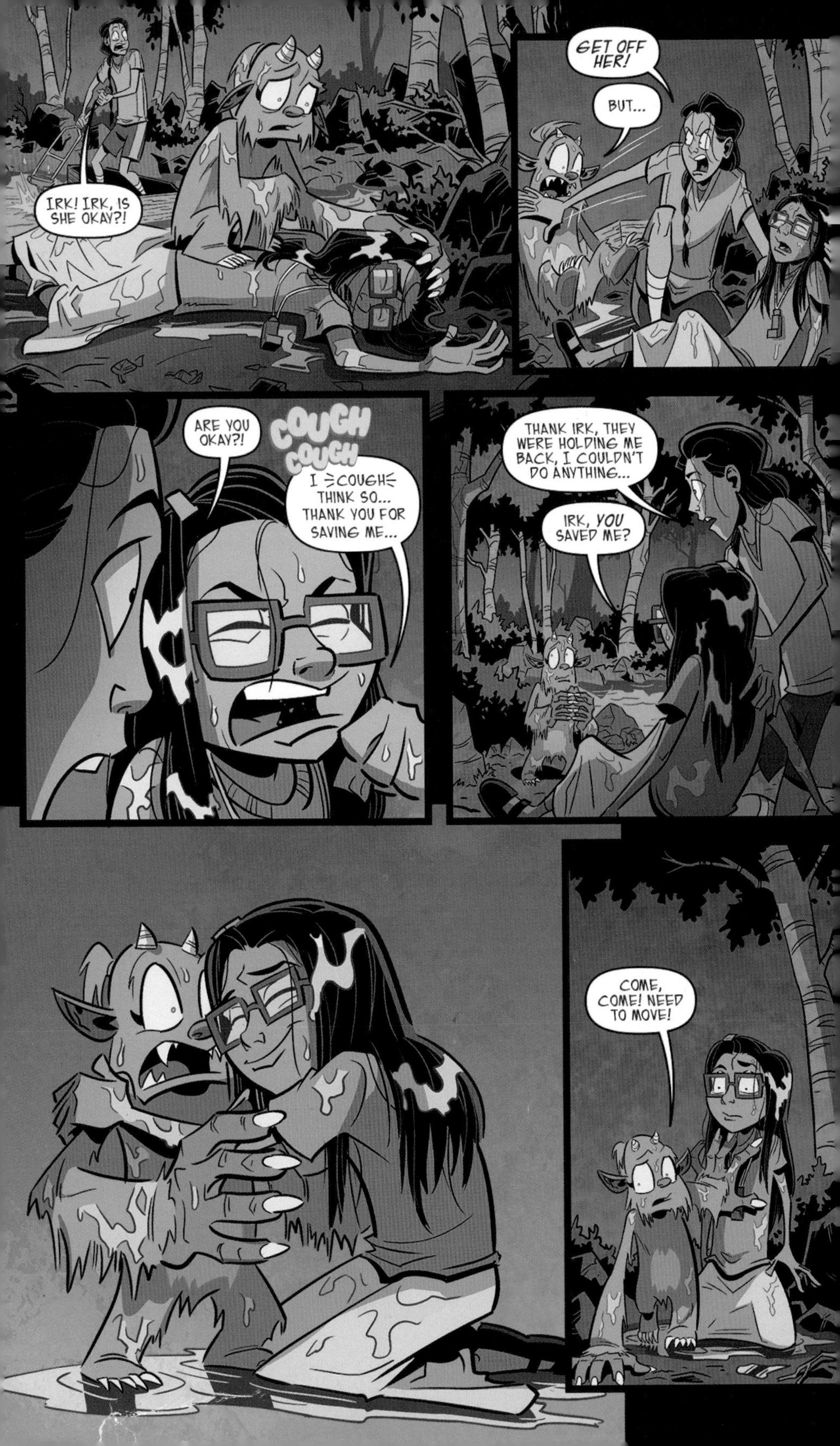
IRK! IRK, IS SHE OKAY?!
GET OFF HER!
BUT...
ARE YOU OKAY?!
COUGH COUGH
I ≡COUGH≡ THINK SO... THANK YOU FOR SAVING ME...
THANK IRK, THEY WERE HOLDING ME BACK, I COULDN'T DO ANYTHING...
IRK, YOU SAVED ME?
COME, COME! NEED TO MOVE!

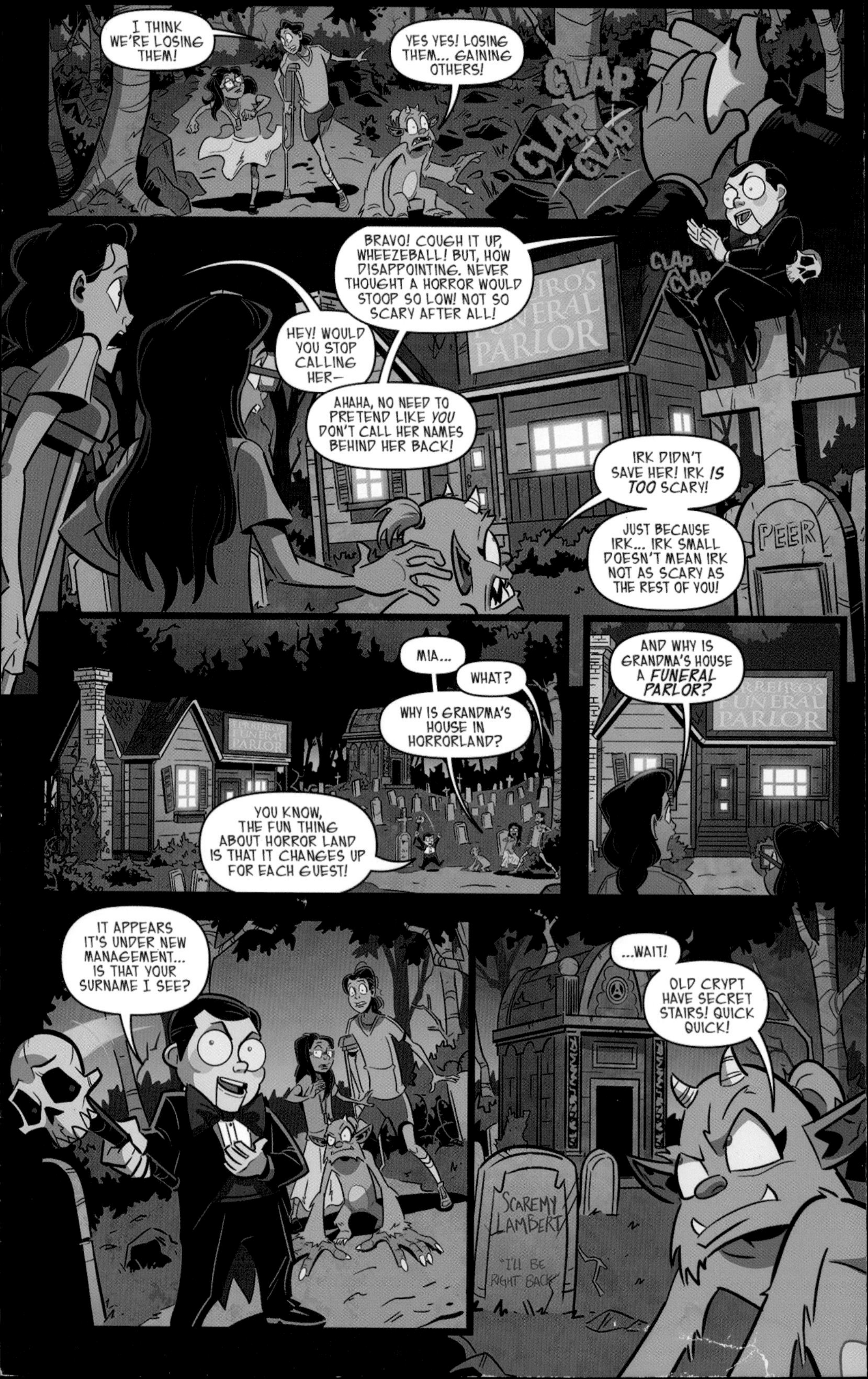
I THINK WE'RE LOSING THEM!
YES YES! LOSING THEM... GAINING OTHERS!
CLAP
CLAP
CLAP
CLAP
BRAVO! COUGH IT UP, WHEEZEBALL! BUT, HOW DISAPPOINTING. NEVER THOUGHT A HORROR WOULD STOOP SO LOW! NOT SO SCARY AFTER ALL!
CLAP
CLAP
HEY! WOULD YOU STOP CALLING HER—
AHAHA, NO NEED TO PRETEND LIKE *YOU* DON'T CALL HER NAMES BEHIND HER BACK!
PARLOR
IRK DIDN'T SAVE HER! IRK *IS TOO* SCARY!
JUST BECAUSE IRK... IRK SMALL DOESN'T MEAN IRK NOT AS SCARY AS THE REST OF YOU!
PEER
MIA...
WHAT?
WHY IS GRANDMA'S HOUSE IN HORRORLAND?
PARLOR
YOU KNOW, THE FUN THING ABOUT HORROR LAND IS THAT IT CHANGES UP FOR EACH GUEST!
AND WHY IS GRANDMA'S HOUSE A *FUNERAL PARLOR?*
PARLOR
IT APPEARS IT'S UNDER NEW MANAGEMENT... IS THAT YOUR SURNAME I SEE?
...WAIT!
OLD CRYPT HAVE SECRET STAIRS! QUICK QUICK!
SCAREMY LAMBERT
"I'LL BE RIGHT BACK"

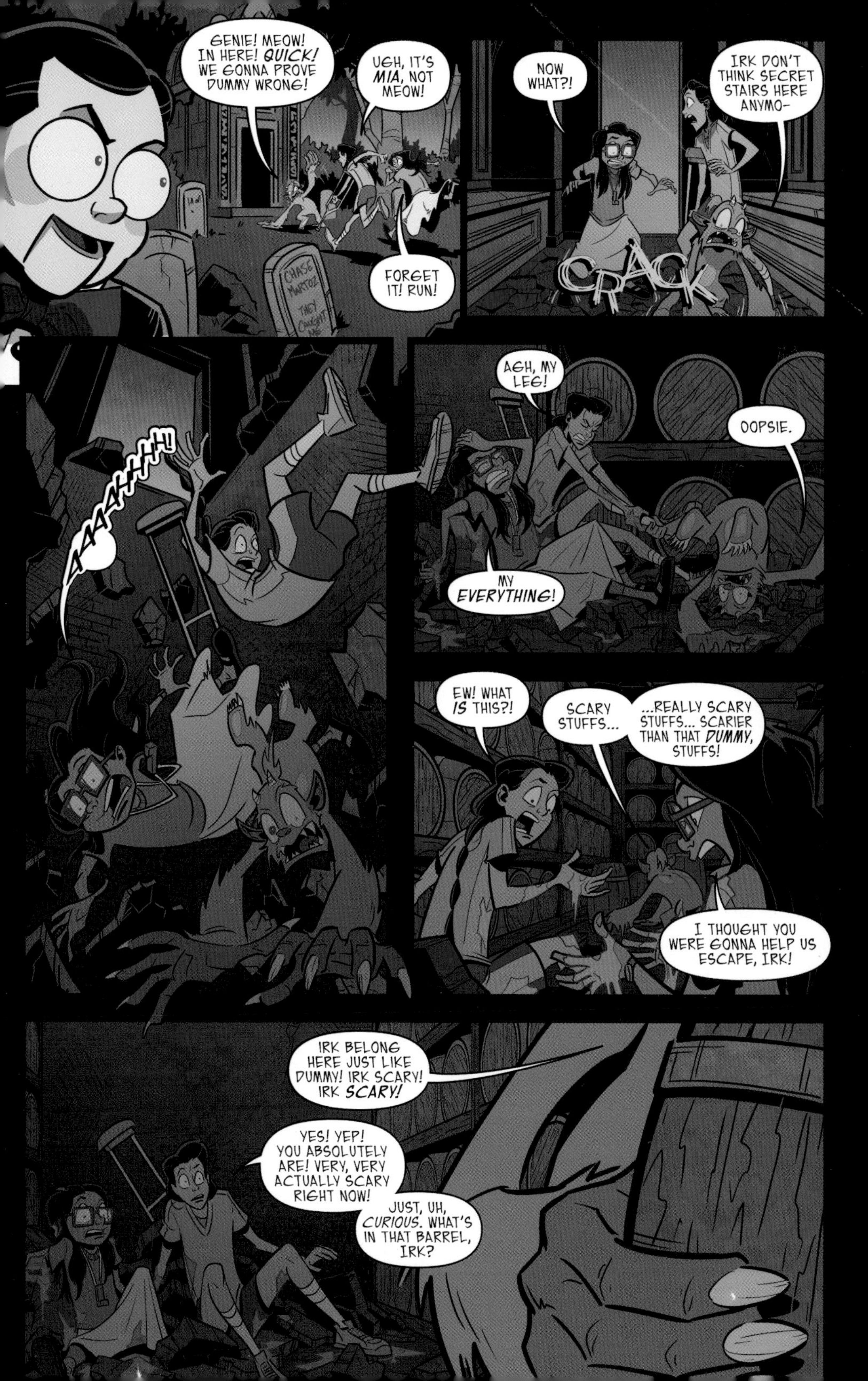
GENIE! MEOW! IN HERE! QUICK! WE GONNA PROVE DUMMY WRONG!
UGH, IT'S MIA, NOT MEOW!
FORGET IT! RUN!
CHASE MARTOZ THEY CAUGHT ME
NOW WHAT?!
IRK DON'T THINK SECRET STAIRS HERE ANYMO-
CRACK
AAAAHHHH!
AGH, MY LEG!
OOPSIE.
MY EVERYTHING!
EW! WHAT IS THIS?!
SCARY STUFFS...
...REALLY SCARY STUFFS... SCARIER THAN THAT DUMMY, STUFFS!
I THOUGHT YOU WERE GONNA HELP US ESCAPE, IRK!
IRK BELONG HERE JUST LIKE DUMMY! IRK SCARY! IRK SCARY!
YES! YEP! YOU ABSOLUTELY ARE! VERY, VERY ACTUALLY SCARY RIGHT NOW!
JUST, UH, CURIOUS. WHAT'S IN THAT BARREL, IRK?

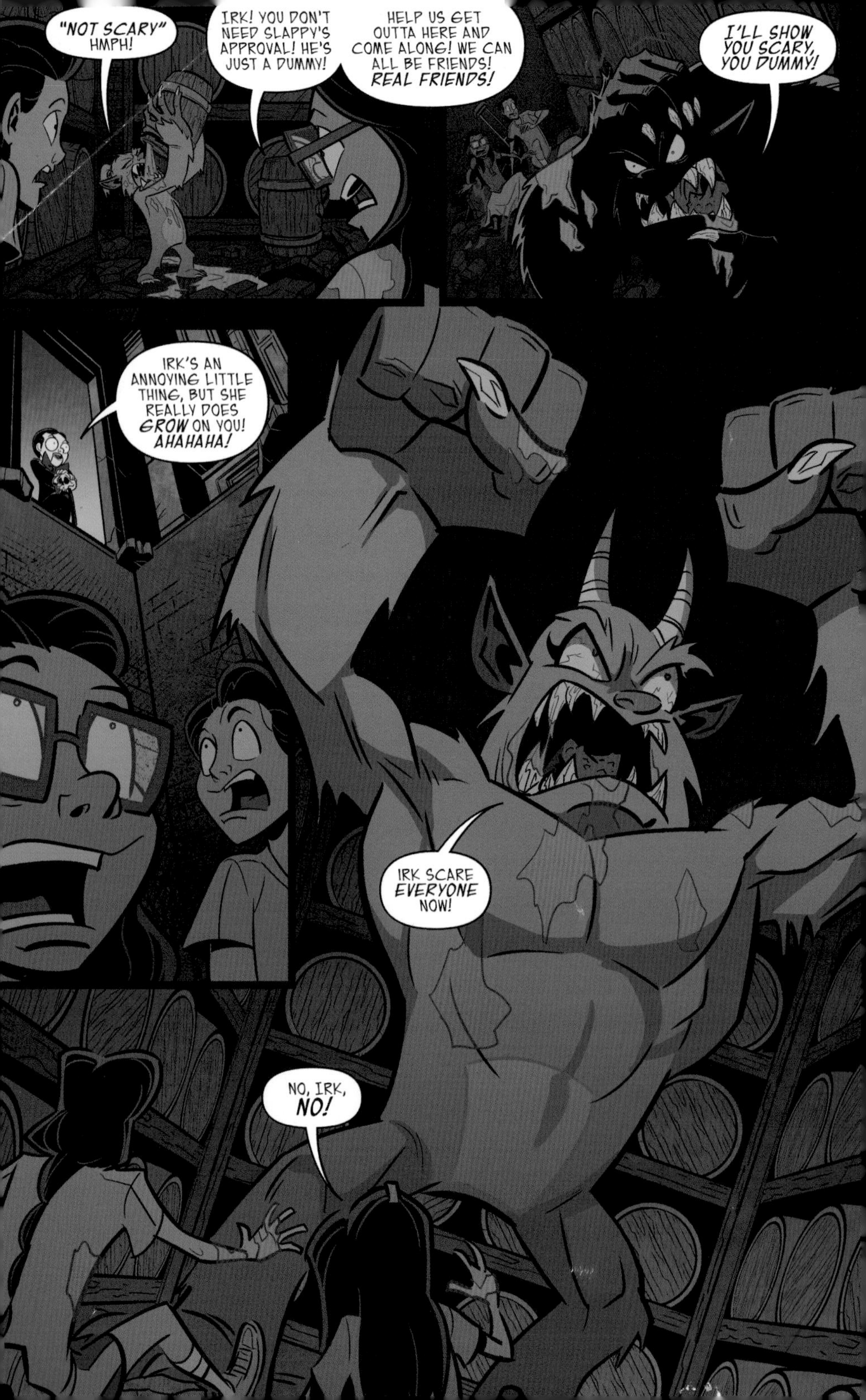
"NOT SCARY" HMPH!
IRK! YOU DON'T NEED SLAPPY'S APPROVAL! HE'S JUST A DUMMY!
HELP US GET OUTTA HERE AND COME ALONG! WE CAN ALL BE FRIENDS! REAL FRIENDS!
I'LL SHOW YOU SCARY, YOU DUMMY!
IRK'S AN ANNOYING LITTLE THING, BUT SHE REALLY DOES GROW ON YOU! AHAHAHA!
IRK SCARE EVERYONE NOW!
NO, IRK, NO!

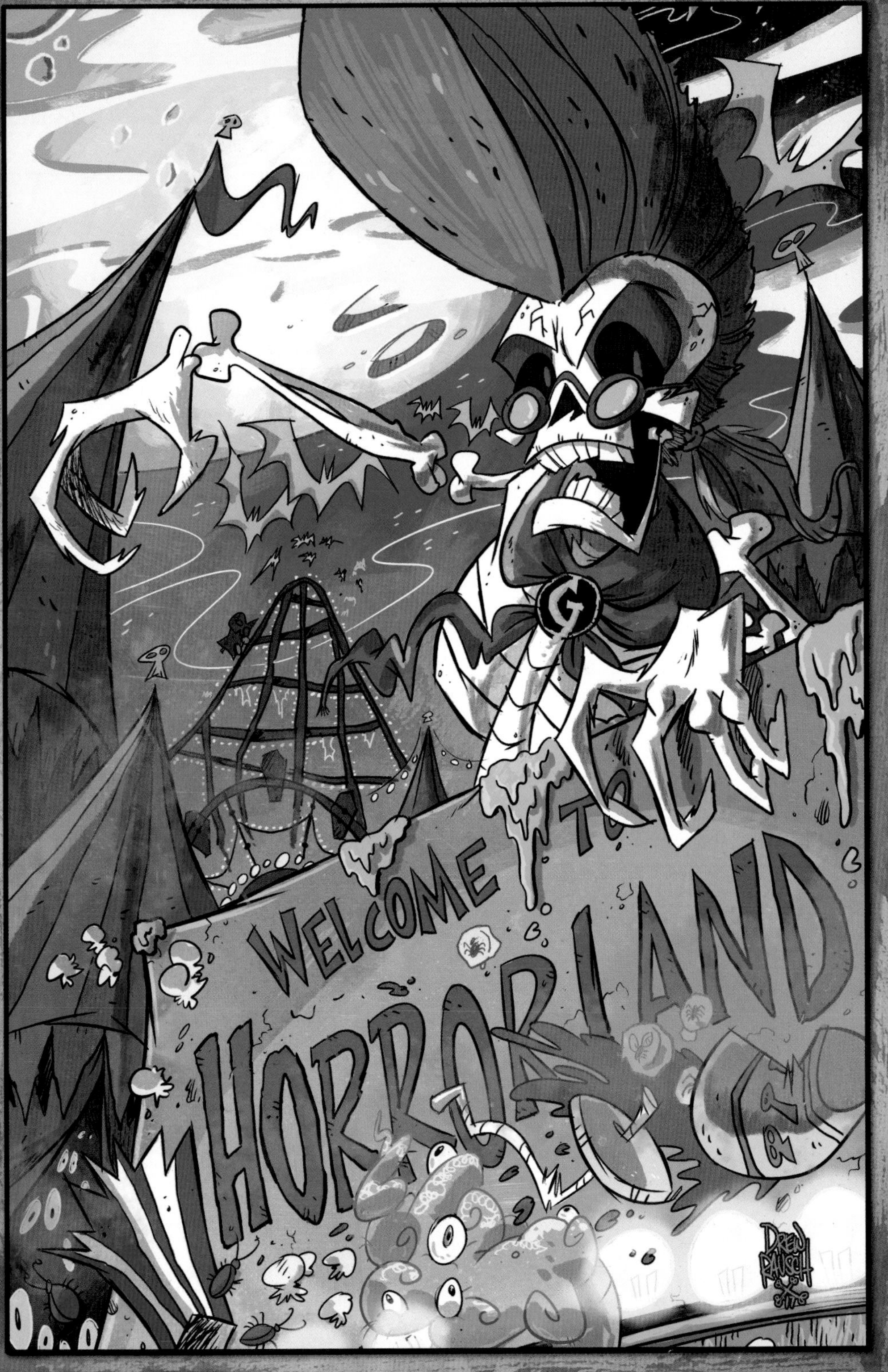
WELCOME TO
HORRORLAND
DREW RAUSCH

ART BY
DREW RAUSCH

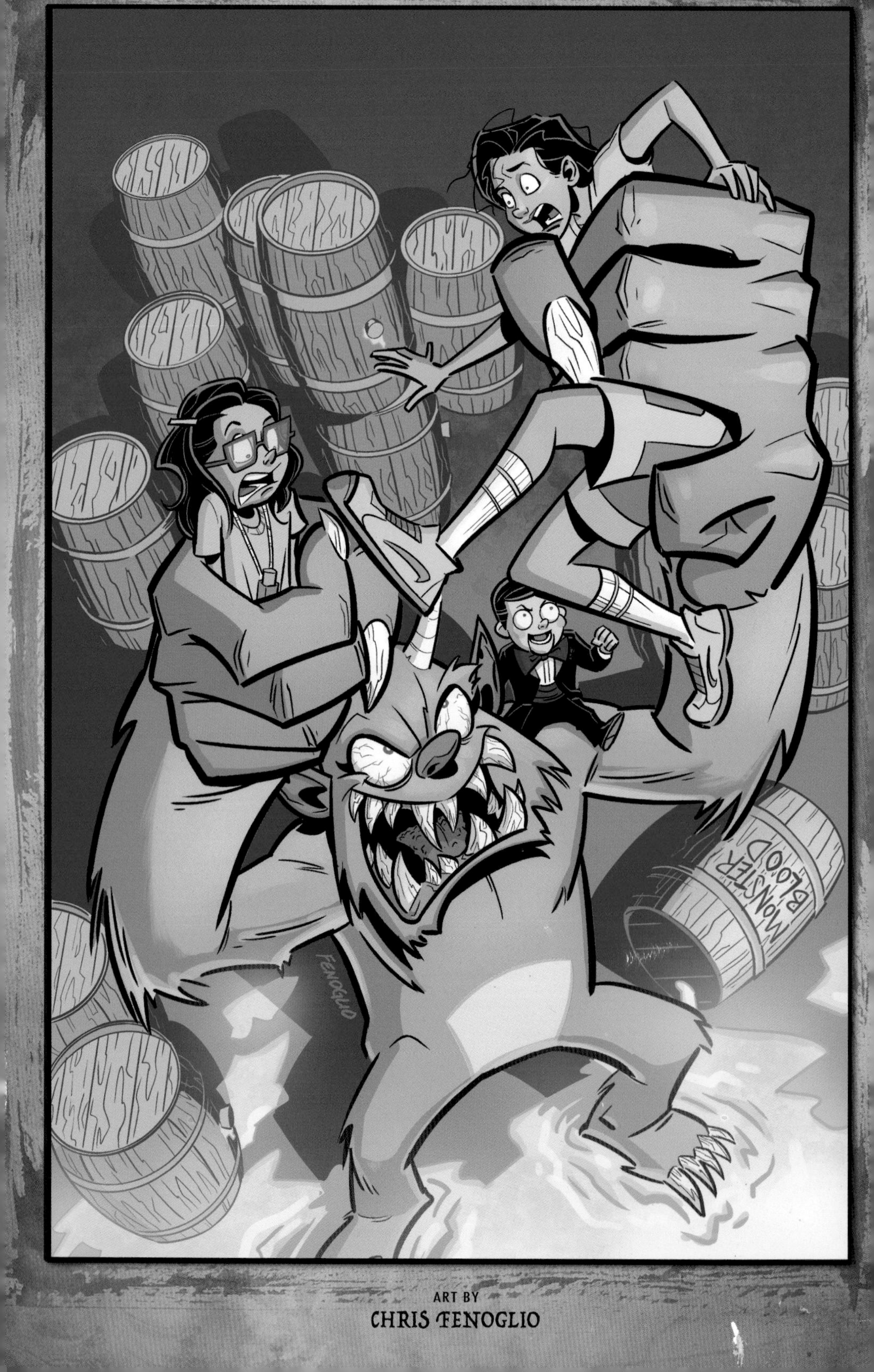
MONSTER BLOOD
FENOGLIO

ART BY
CHRIS FENOGLIO

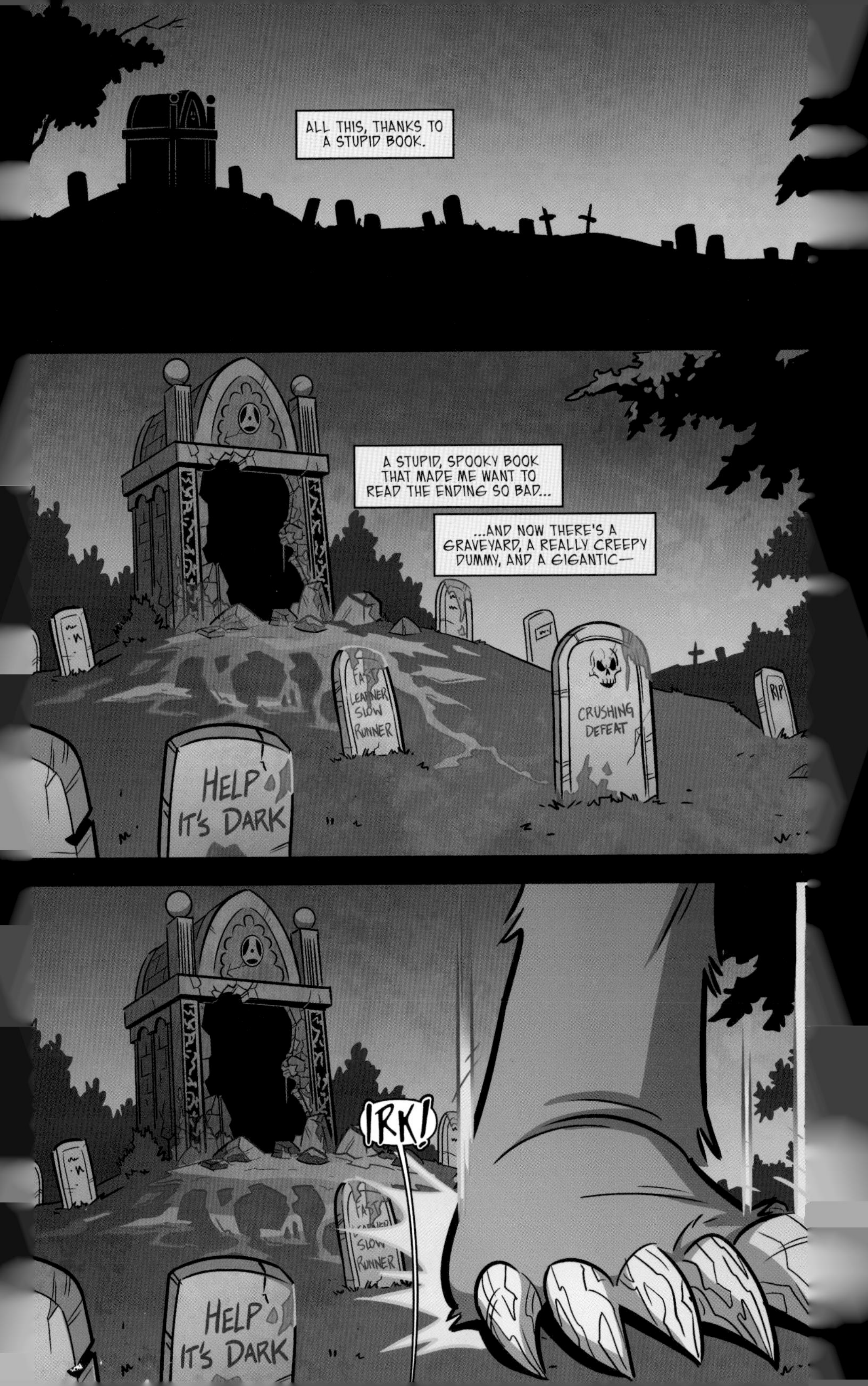
ALL THIS, THANKS TO A STUPID BOOK.
A STUPID, SPOOKY BOOK THAT MADE ME WANT TO READ THE ENDING SO BAD...
...AND NOW THERE'S A GRAVEYARD, A REALLY CREEPY DUMMY, AND A GIGANTIC—
FAST LEARNER SLOW RUNNER
CRUSHING DEFEAT
RIP
HELP IT'S DARK
IRK!
HELP IT'S DARK

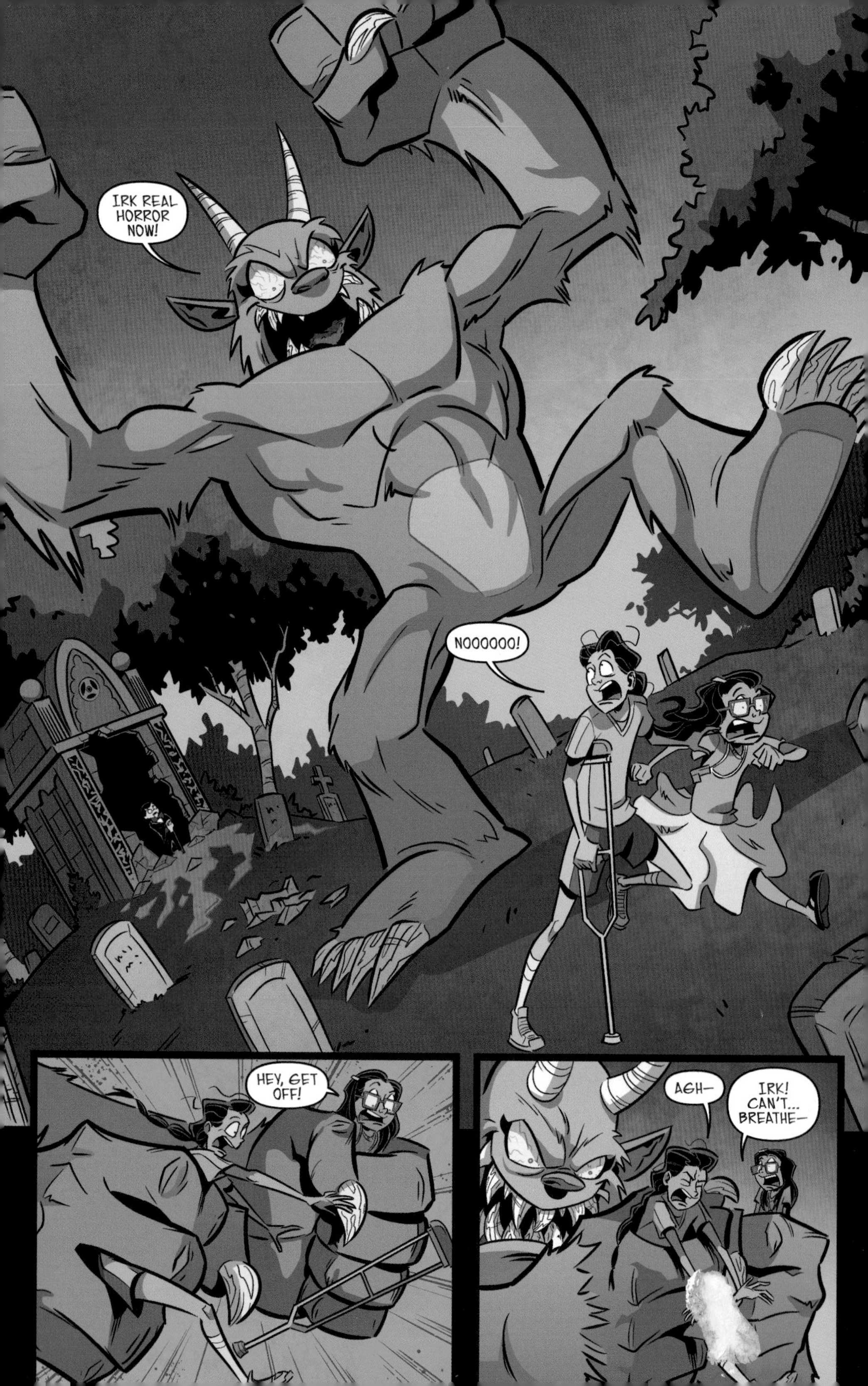
IRK REAL HORROR NOW!
NOOOOOO!
HEY, GET OFF!
AGH—
IRK! CAN'T... BREATHE—

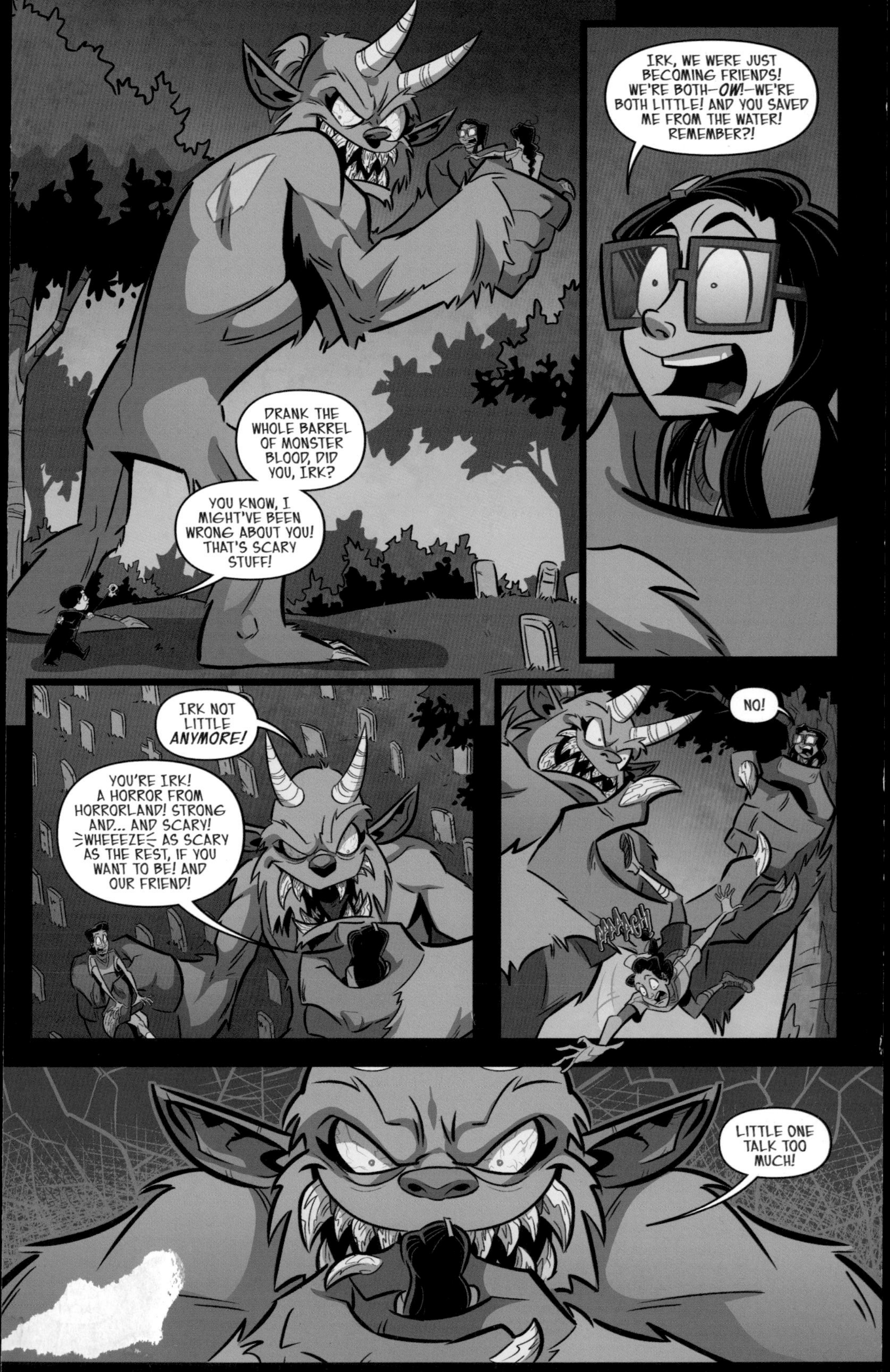
IRK, WE WERE JUST BECOMING FRIENDS! WE'RE BOTH—OW!—WE'RE BOTH LITTLE! AND YOU SAVED ME FROM THE WATER! REMEMBER?!
DRANK THE WHOLE BARREL OF MONSTER BLOOD, DID YOU, IRK?
YOU KNOW, I MIGHT'VE BEEN WRONG ABOUT YOU! THAT'S SCARY STUFF!
IRK NOT LITTLE ANYMORE!
YOU'RE IRK! A HORROR FROM HORRORLAND! STRONG AND... AND SCARY! WHEEEZE AS SCARY AS THE REST, IF YOU WANT TO BE! AND OUR FRIEND!
NO!
AAAAGH!
LITTLE ONE TALK TOO MUCH!

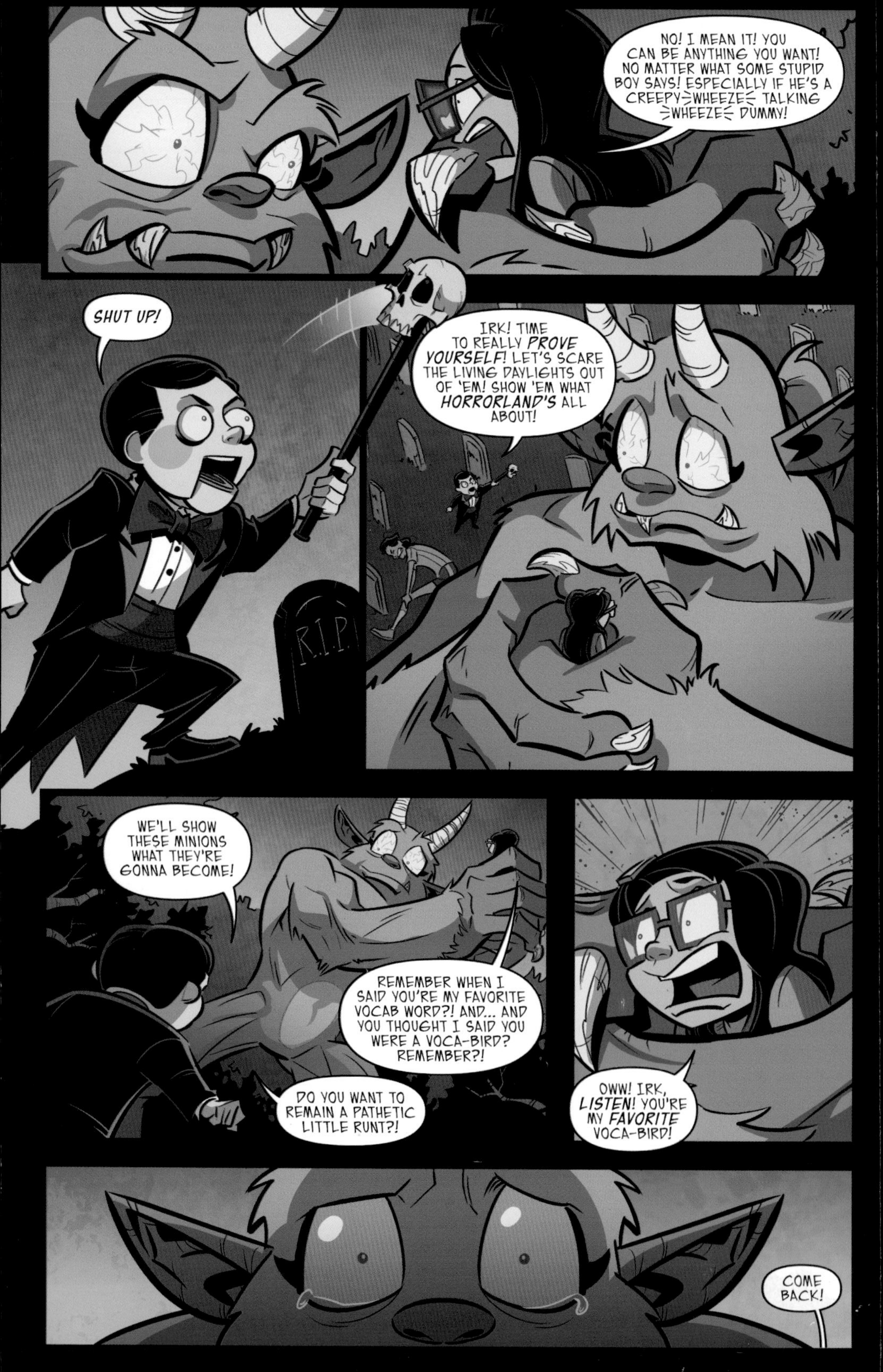
NO! I MEAN IT! YOU CAN BE ANYTHING YOU WANT! NO MATTER WHAT SOME STUPID BOY SAYS! ESPECIALLY IF HE'S A CREEPY *WHEEZE* TALKING *WHEEZE* DUMMY!
SHUT UP!
IRK! TIME TO REALLY PROVE YOURSELF! LET'S SCARE THE LIVING DAYLIGHTS OUT OF 'EM! SHOW 'EM WHAT HORRORLAND'S ALL ABOUT!
R.I.P.
WE'LL SHOW THESE MINIONS WHAT THEY'RE GONNA BECOME!
REMEMBER WHEN I SAID YOU'RE MY FAVORITE VOCAB WORD?! AND... AND YOU THOUGHT I SAID YOU WERE A VOCA-BIRD? REMEMBER?!
DO YOU WANT TO REMAIN A PATHETIC LITTLE RUNT?!
OWW! IRK, LISTEN! YOU'RE MY FAVORITE VOCA-BIRD!
COME BACK!

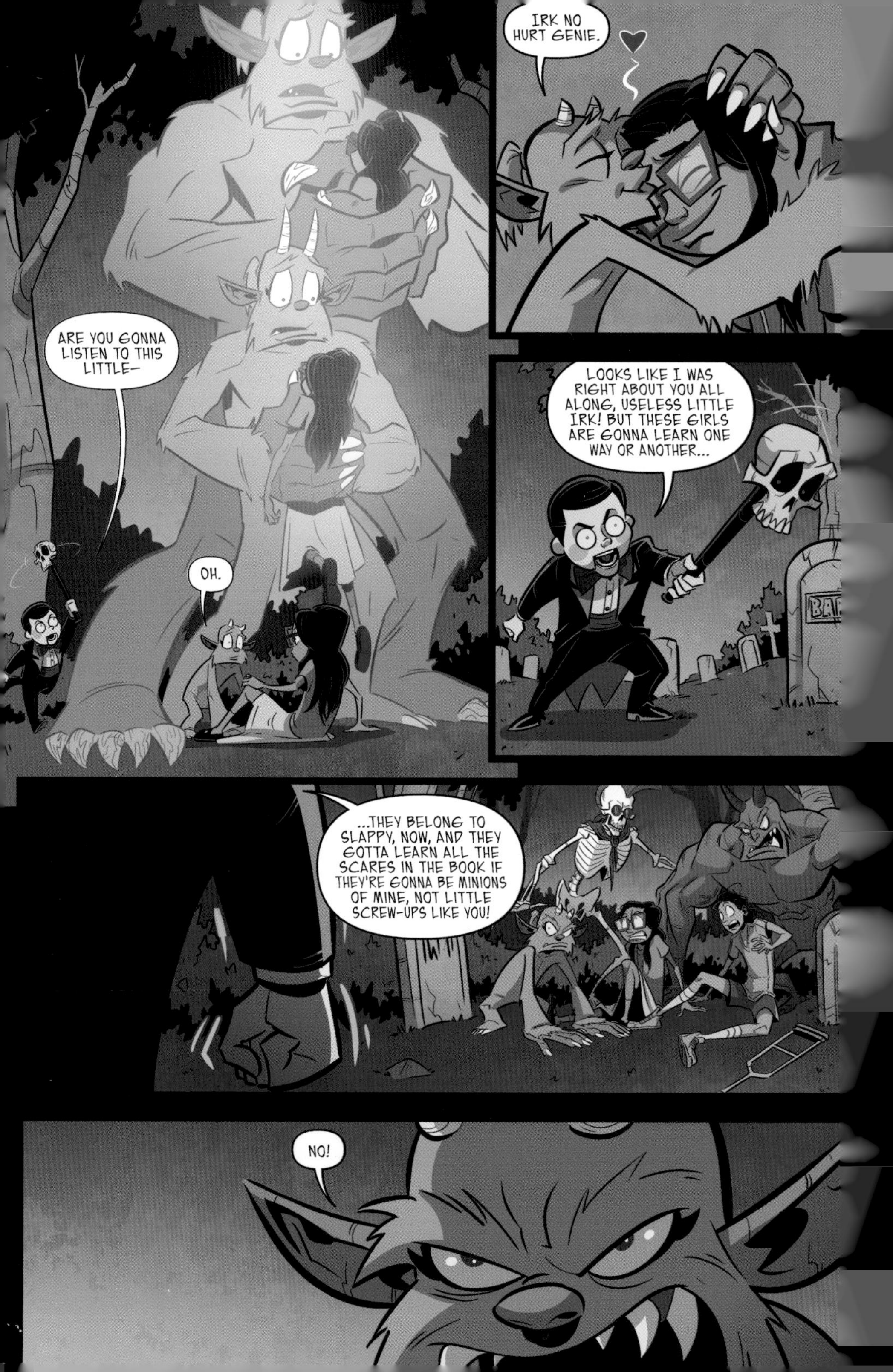
ARE YOU GONNA LISTEN TO THIS LITTLE–
OH.
IRK NO HURT GENIE.
LOOKS LIKE I WAS RIGHT ABOUT YOU ALL ALONG, USELESS LITTLE IRK! BUT THESE GIRLS ARE GONNA LEARN ONE WAY OR ANOTHER...
...THEY BELONG TO SLAPPY, NOW, AND THEY GOTTA LEARN ALL THE SCARES IN THE BOOK IF THEY'RE GONNA BE MINIONS OF MINE, NOT LITTLE SCREW-UPS LIKE YOU!
NO!

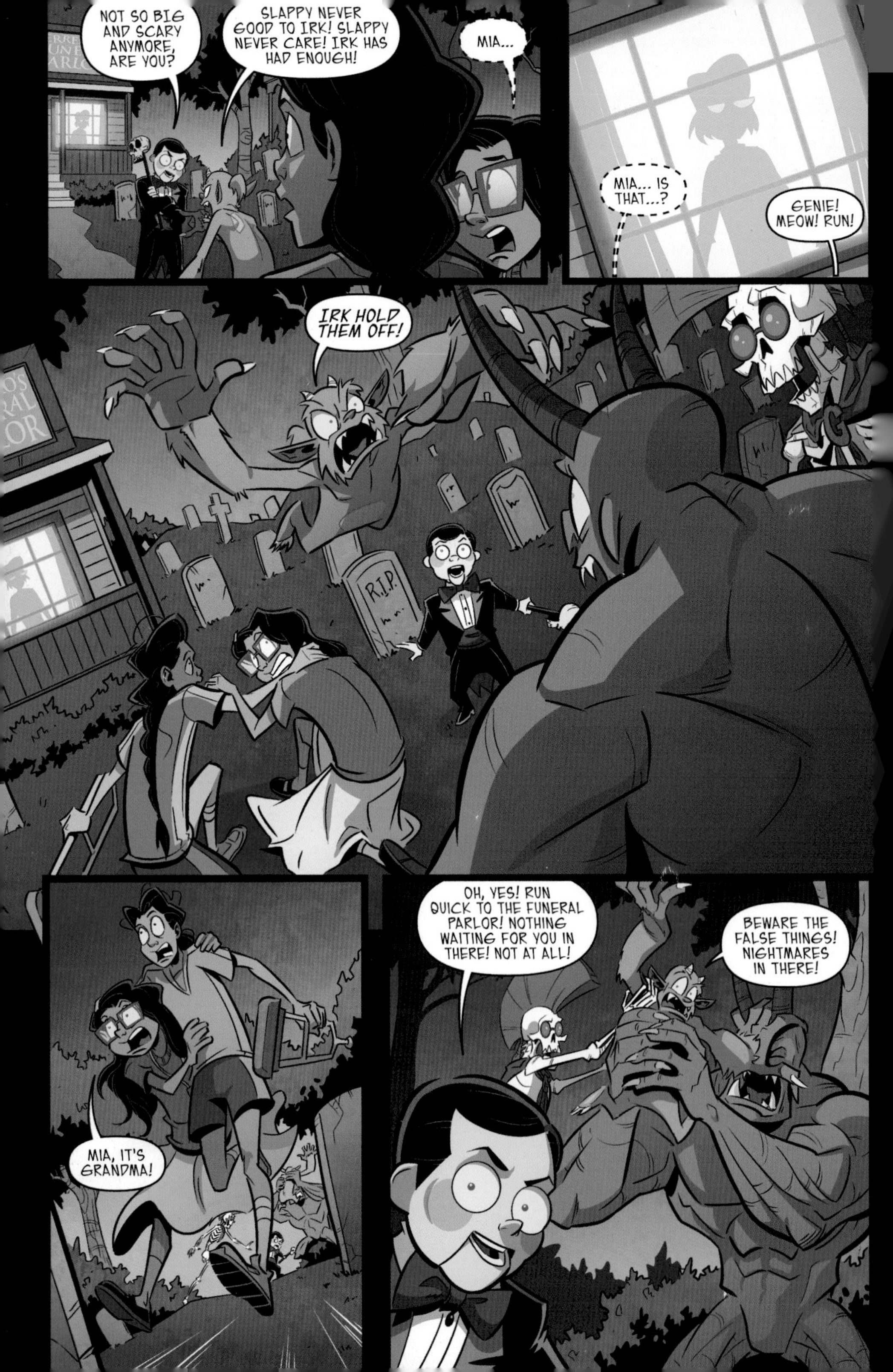
NOT SO BIG AND SCARY ANYMORE, ARE YOU?
SLAPPY NEVER GOOD TO IRK! SLAPPY NEVER CARE! IRK HAS HAD ENOUGH!
MIA...
MIA... IS THAT...?
GENIE! MEOW! RUN!
IRK HOLD THEM OFF!
R.I.P.
MIA, IT'S GRANDMA!
OH, YES! RUN QUICK TO THE FUNERAL PARLOR! NOTHING WAITING FOR YOU IN THERE! NOT AT ALL!
BEWARE THE FALSE THINGS! NIGHTMARES IN THERE!

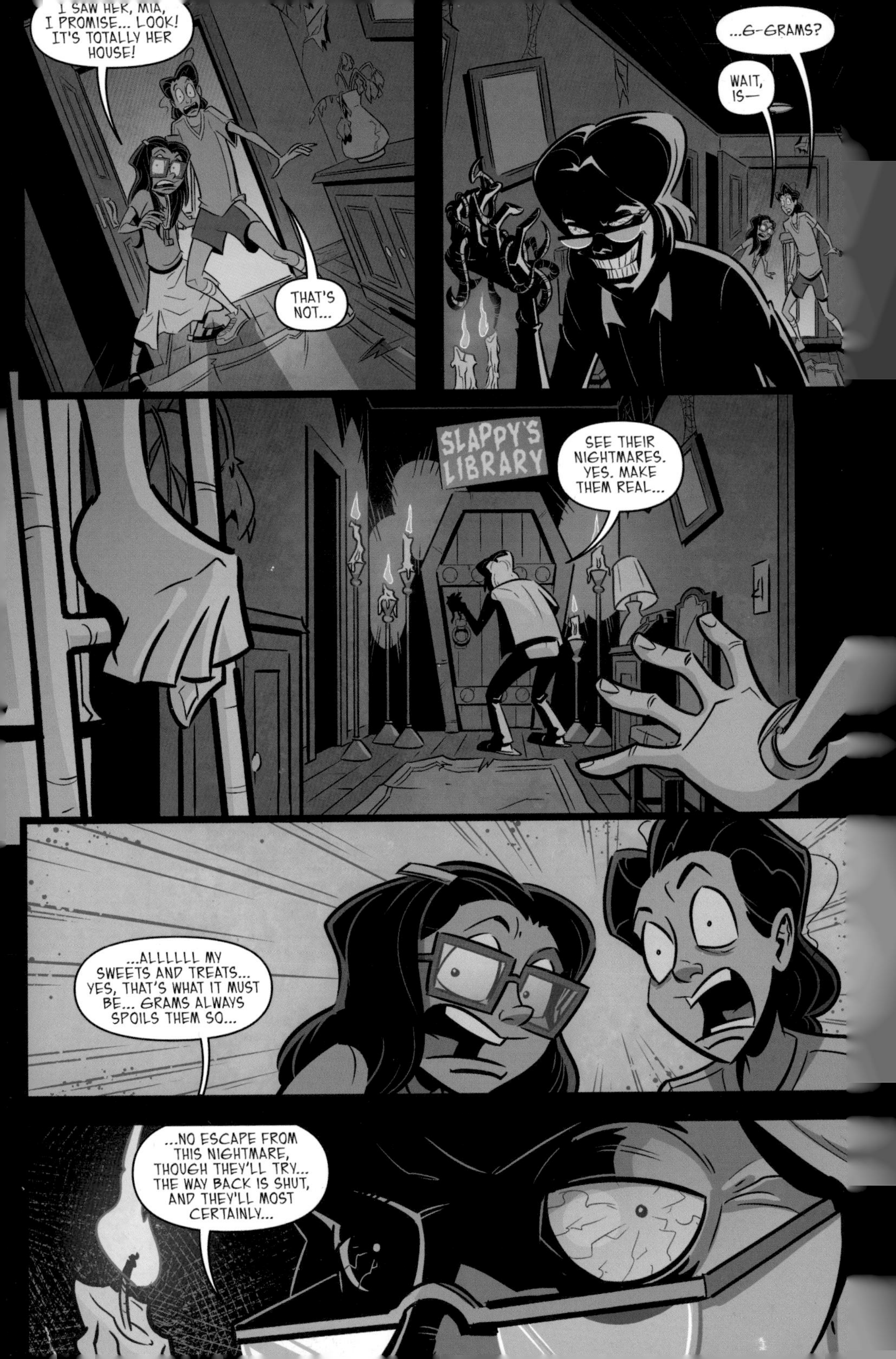
I SAW HER, MIA, I PROMISE... LOOK! IT'S TOTALLY HER HOUSE!
THAT'S NOT...
...G-GRAMS?
WAIT, IS—
SLAPPY'S LIBRARY
SEE THEIR NIGHTMARES. YES. MAKE THEM REAL...
...ALLLLLL MY SWEETS AND TREATS... YES, THAT'S WHAT IT MUST BE... GRAMS ALWAYS SPOILS THEM SO...
...NO ESCAPE FROM THIS NIGHTMARE, THOUGH THEY'LL TRY... THE WAY BACK IS SHUT, AND THEY'LL MOST CERTAINLY...

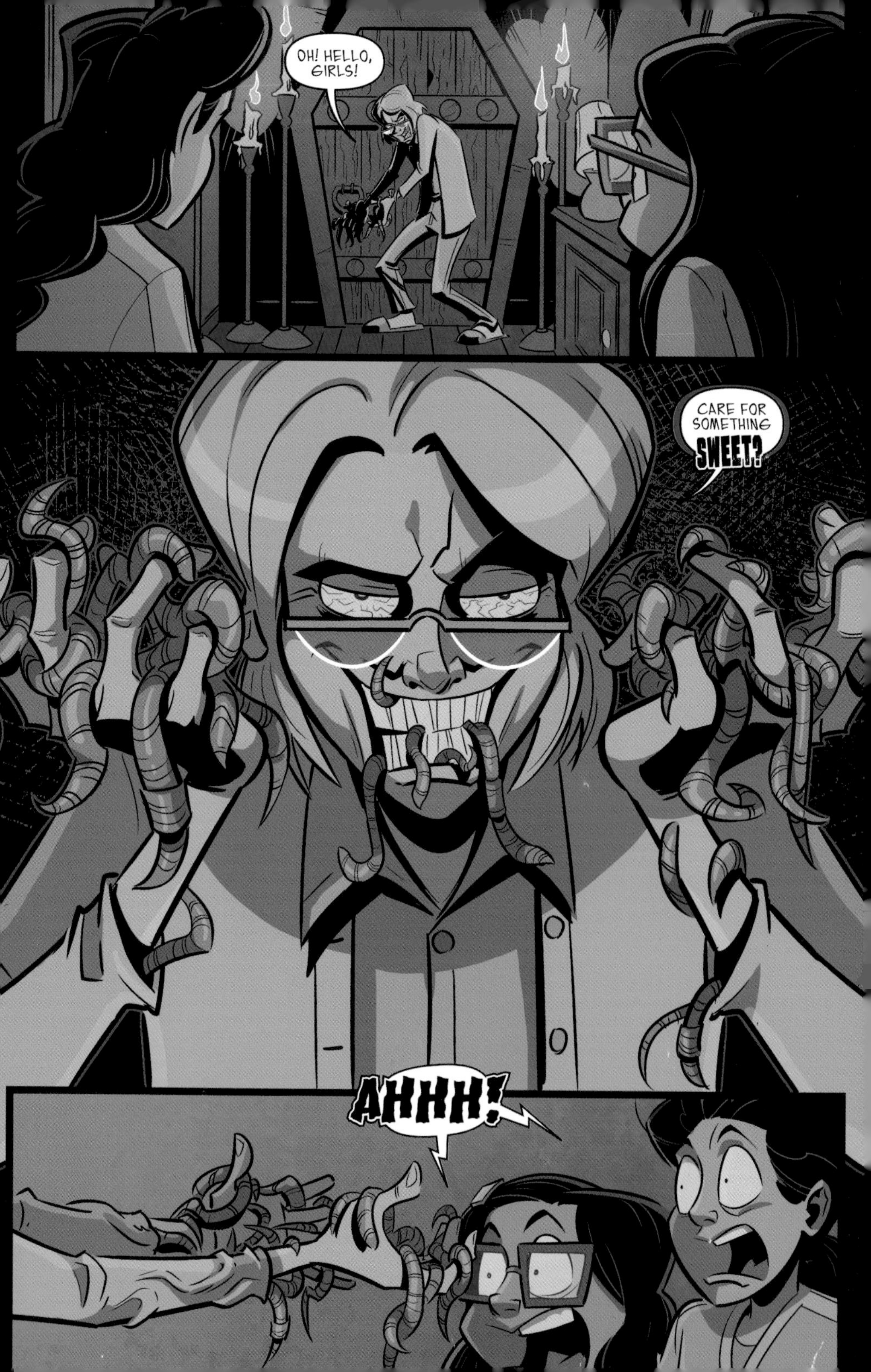
OH! HELLO, GIRLS!
CARE FOR SOMETHING SWEET?
AHHH!

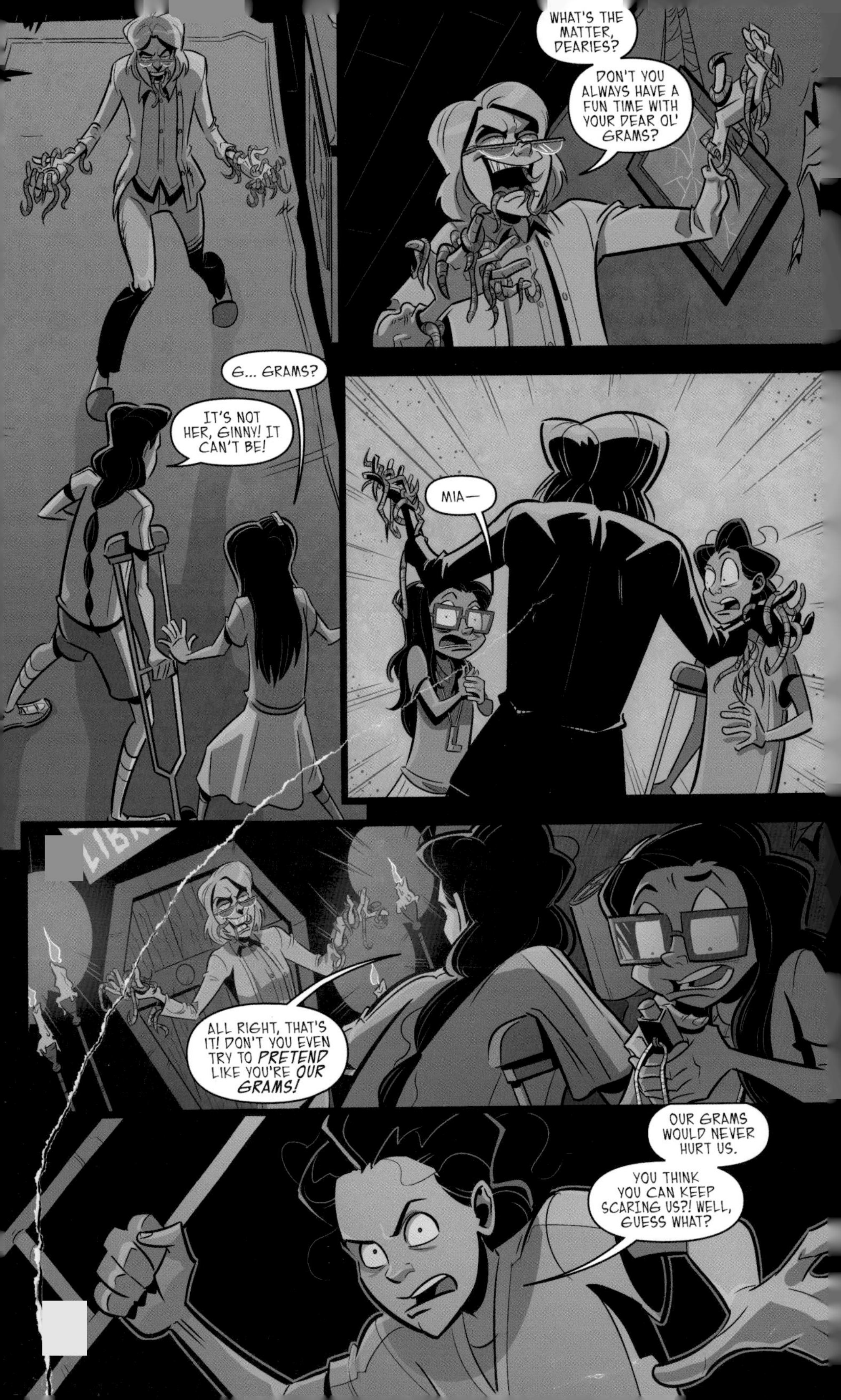
WHAT'S THE MATTER, DEARIES?
DON'T YOU ALWAYS HAVE A FUN TIME WITH YOUR DEAR OL' GRAMS?
G... GRAMS?
IT'S NOT HER, GINNY! IT CAN'T BE!
MIA—
ALL RIGHT, THAT'S IT! DON'T YOU EVEN TRY TO PRETEND LIKE YOU'RE OUR GRAMS!
OUR GRAMS WOULD NEVER HURT US.
YOU THINK YOU CAN KEEP SCARING US?! WELL, GUESS WHAT?

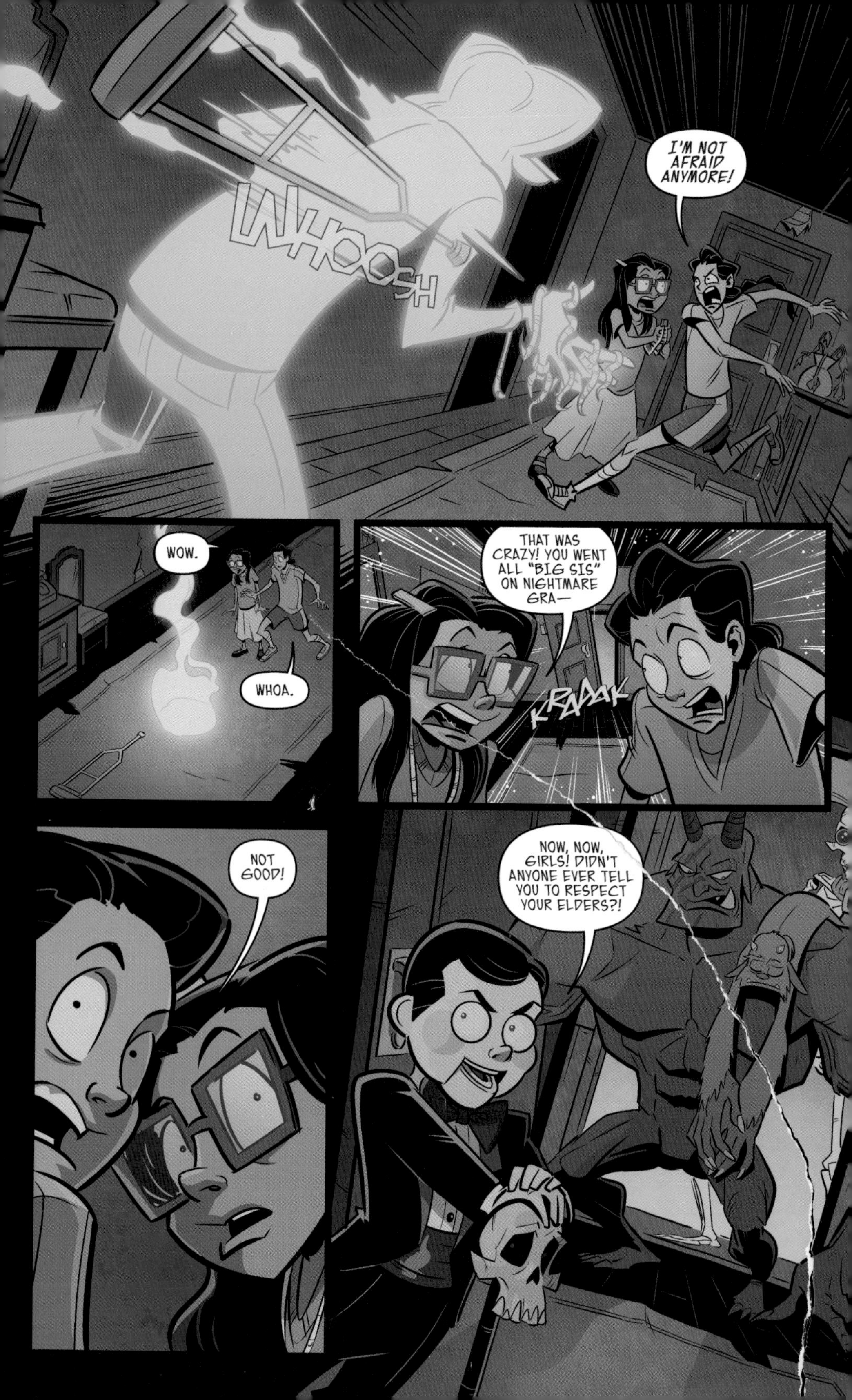
WHOOSH
I'M NOT AFRAID ANYMORE!
WOW.
WHOA.
THAT WAS CRAZY! YOU WENT ALL "BIG SIS" ON NIGHTMARE GRA—
KRADAK
NOT GOOD!
NOW, NOW, GIRLS! DIDN'T ANYONE EVER TELL YOU TO RESPECT YOUR ELDERS?!

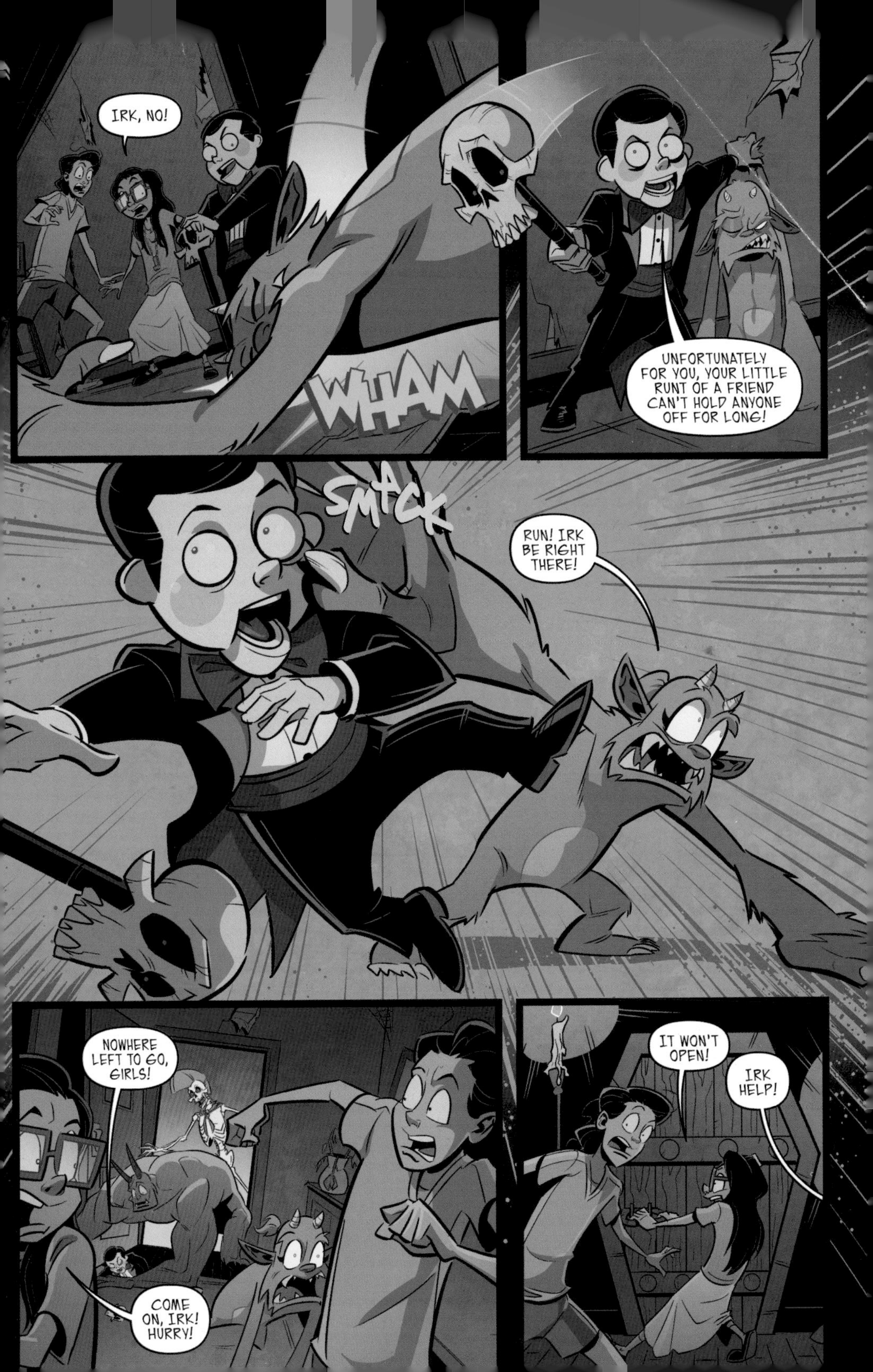
IRK, NO!
WHAM
UNFORTUNATELY FOR YOU, YOUR LITTLE RUNT OF A FRIEND CAN'T HOLD ANYONE OFF FOR LONG!
SMACK
RUN! IRK BE RIGHT THERE!
NOWHERE LEFT TO GO, GIRLS!
COME ON, IRK! HURRY!
IT WON'T OPEN!
IRK HELP!

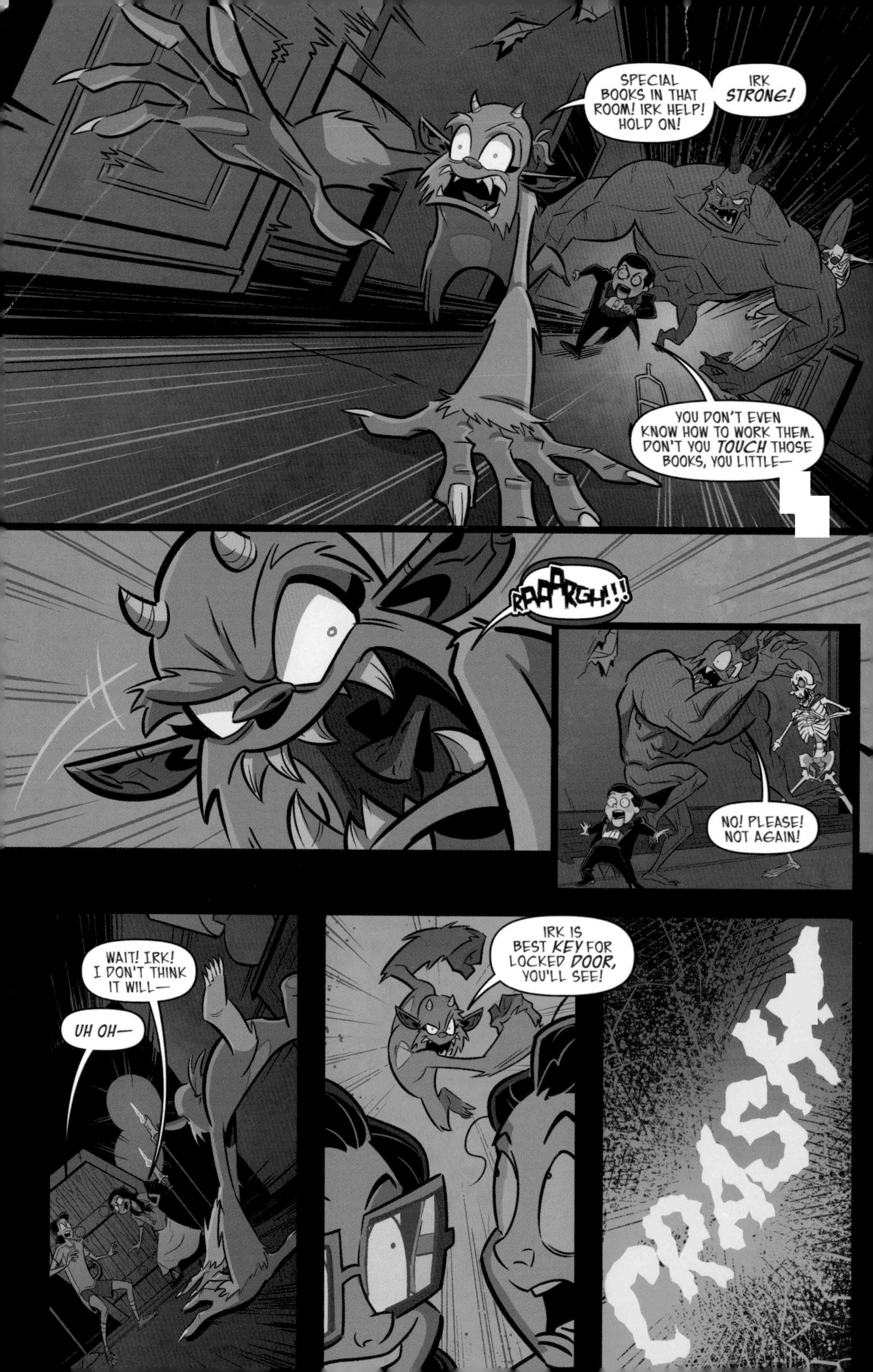

SPECIAL BOOKS IN THAT ROOM! IRK HELP! HOLD ON!
IRK STRONG!
YOU DON'T EVEN KNOW HOW TO WORK THEM. DON'T YOU TOUCH THOSE BOOKS, YOU LITTLE—
RAAARGH!!!
NO! PLEASE! NOT AGAIN!
WAIT! IRK! I DON'T THINK IT WILL—
UH OH—
IRK IS BEST KEY FOR LOCKED DOOR, YOU'LL SEE!
CRASH!

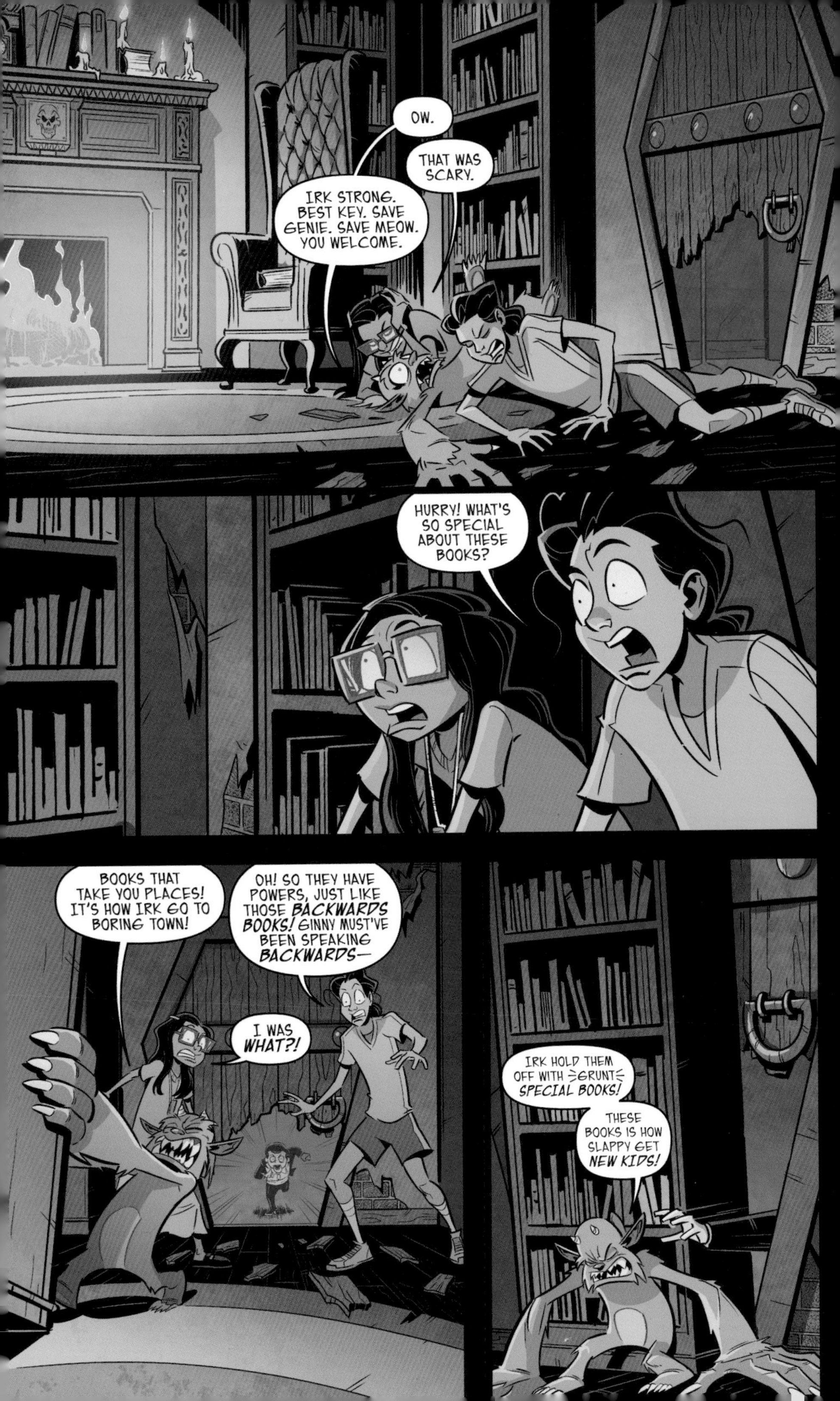

OW.
THAT WAS SCARY.
IRK STRONG. BEST KEY. SAVE GENIE. SAVE MEOW. YOU WELCOME.
HURRY! WHAT'S SO SPECIAL ABOUT THESE BOOKS?
BOOKS THAT TAKE YOU PLACES! IT'S HOW IRK GO TO BORING TOWN!
OH! SO THEY HAVE POWERS, JUST LIKE THOSE BACKWARDS BOOKS! GINNY MUST'VE BEEN SPEAKING BACKWARDS—
I WAS WHAT?!
IRK HOLD THEM OFF WITH GRUNT SPECIAL BOOKS!
THESE BOOKS IS HOW SLAPPY GET NEW KIDS!

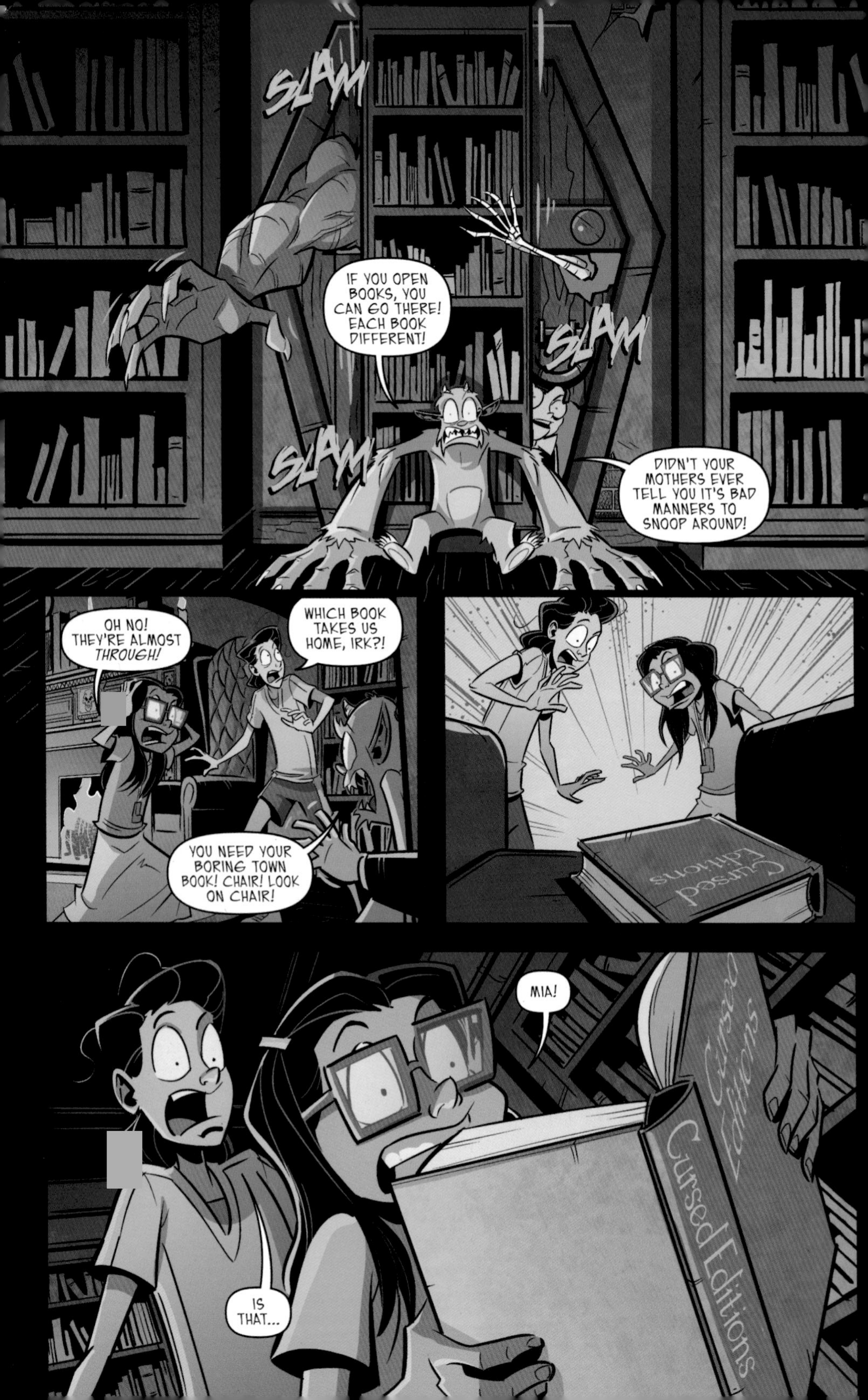
SLAM
IF YOU OPEN BOOKS, YOU CAN GO THERE! EACH BOOK DIFFERENT!
SLAM
SLAM
DIDN'T YOUR MOTHERS EVER TELL YOU IT'S BAD MANNERS TO SNOOP AROUND!
OH NO! THEY'RE ALMOST *THROUGH!*
WHICH BOOK TAKES US HOME, IRK?!
YOU NEED YOUR BORING TOWN BOOK! CHAIR! LOOK ON CHAIR!
Cursed Editions
MIA!
IS THAT...
Cursed Editions
Cursed Editions

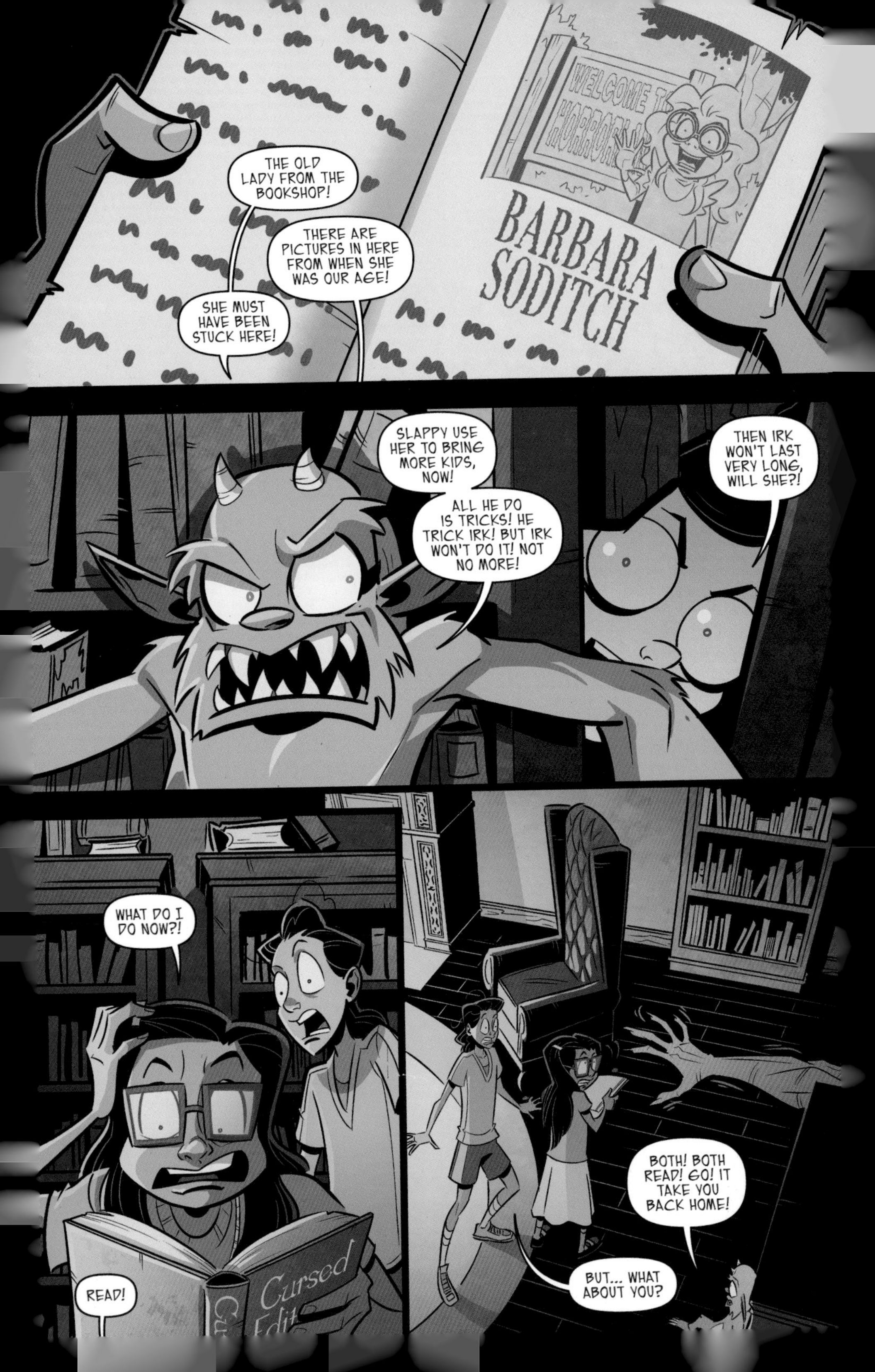
BARBARA SODITCH
THE OLD LADY FROM THE BOOKSHOP!
THERE ARE PICTURES IN HERE FROM WHEN SHE WAS OUR AGE!
SHE MUST HAVE BEEN STUCK HERE!
SLAPPY USE HER TO BRING MORE KIDS, NOW!
ALL HE DO IS TRICKS! HE TRICK IRK! BUT IRK WON'T DO IT! NOT NO MORE!
THEN IRK WON'T LAST VERY LONG, WILL SHE?!
WHAT DO I DO NOW?!
READ!
Cursed
BOTH! BOTH READ! GO! IT TAKE YOU BACK HOME!
BUT... WHAT ABOUT YOU?

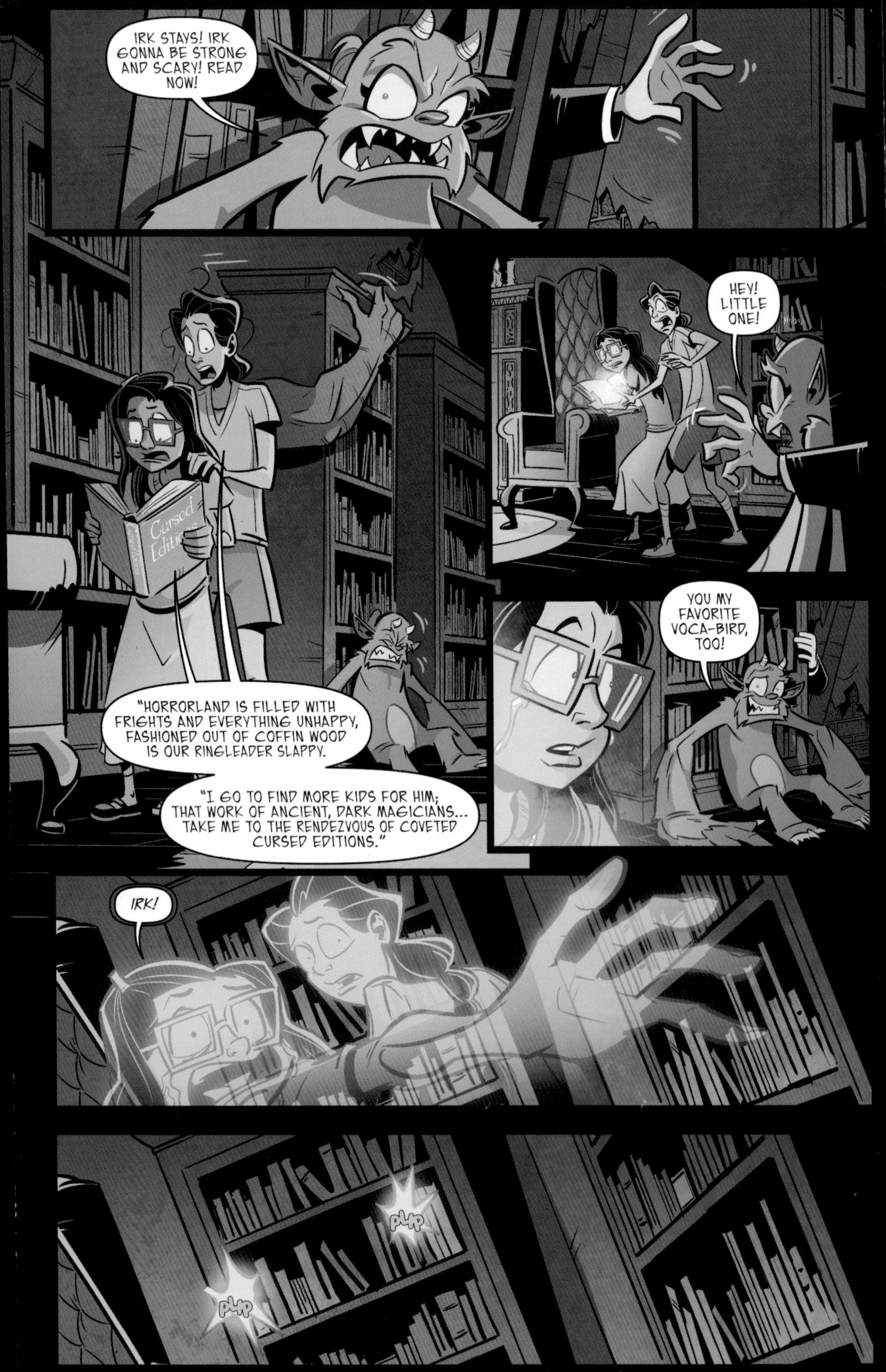
IRK STAYS! IRK GONNA BE STRONG AND SCARY! READ NOW!
Cursed Editions
HEY! LITTLE ONE!
"HORRORLAND IS FILLED WITH FRIGHTS AND EVERYTHING UNHAPPY, FASHIONED OUT OF COFFIN WOOD IS OUR RINGLEADER SLAPPY.
"I GO TO FIND MORE KIDS FOR HIM; THAT WORK OF ANCIENT, DARK MAGICIANS... TAKE ME TO THE RENDEZVOUS OF COVETED CURSED EDITIONS."
YOU MY FAVORITE VOCA-BIRD, TOO!
IRK!
PLIP
PLIP

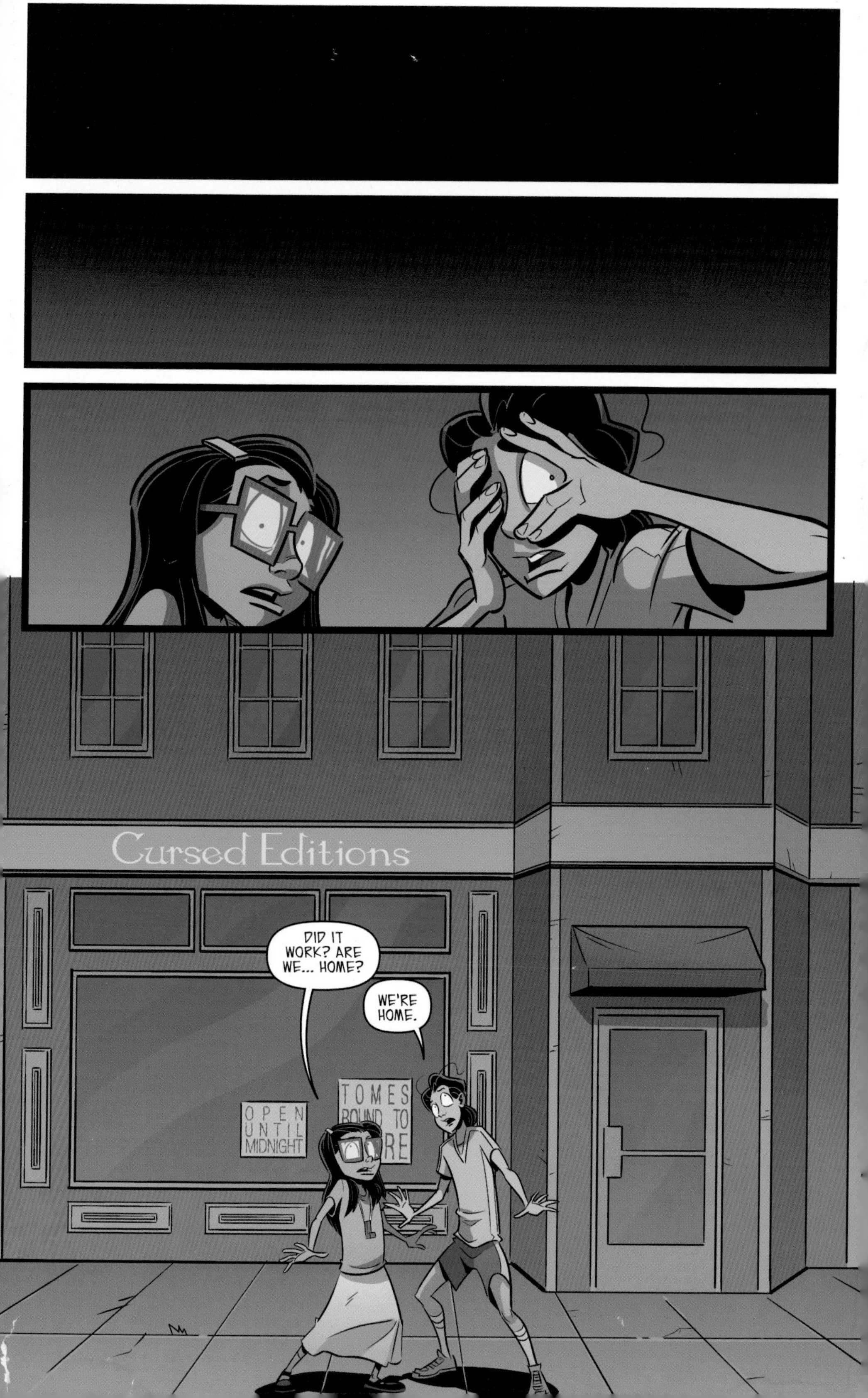
Cursed Editions
DID IT WORK? ARE WE... HOME?
WE'RE HOME.
OPEN UNTIL MIDNIGHT

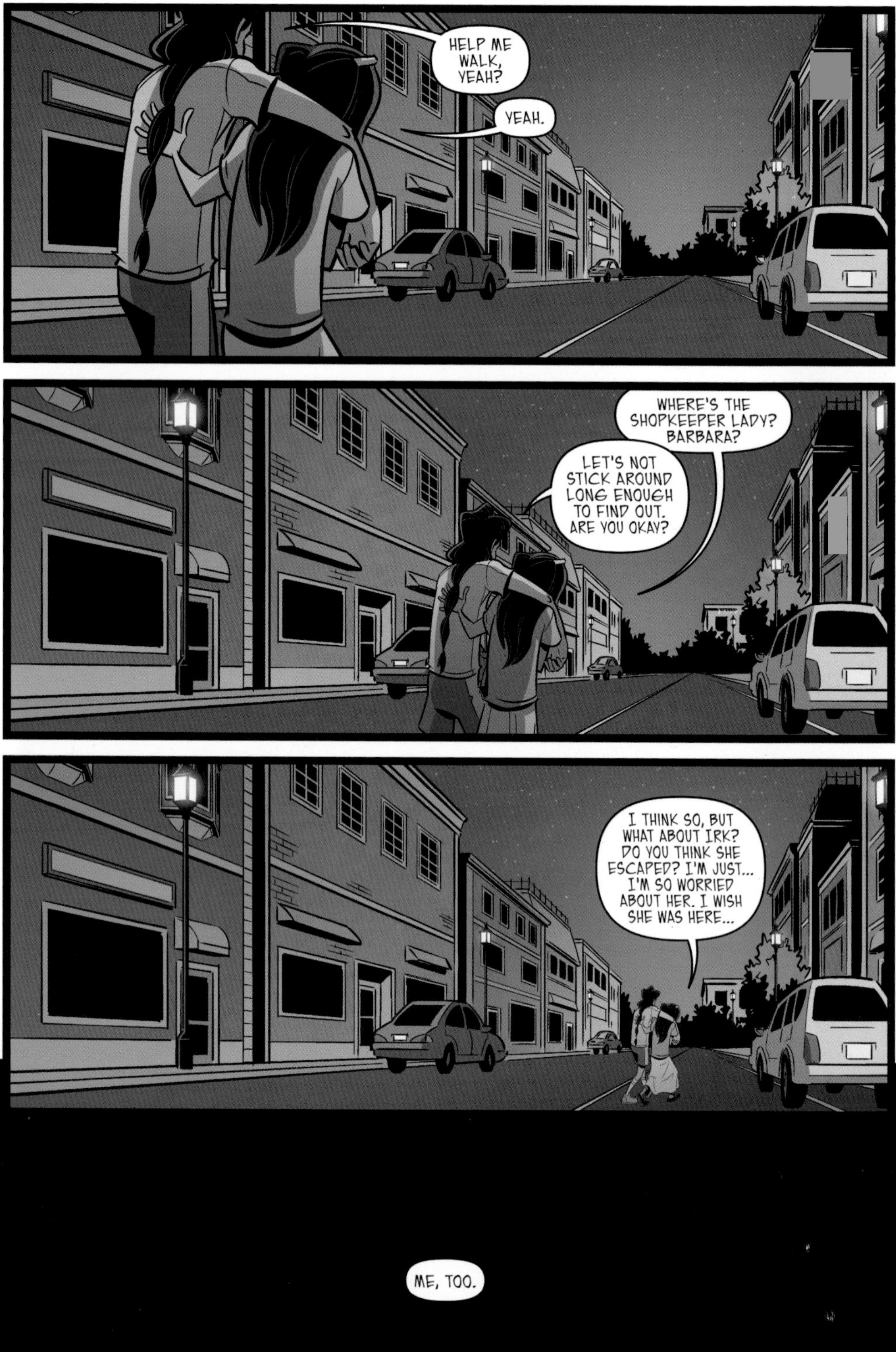
HELP ME WALK, YEAH?
YEAH.
WHERE'S THE SHOPKEEPER LADY? BARBARA?
LET'S NOT STICK AROUND LONG ENOUGH TO FIND OUT. ARE YOU OKAY?
I THINK SO, BUT WHAT ABOUT IRK? DO YOU THINK SHE ESCAPED? I'M JUST... I'M SO WORRIED ABOUT HER. I WISH SHE WAS HERE...
ME, TOO.

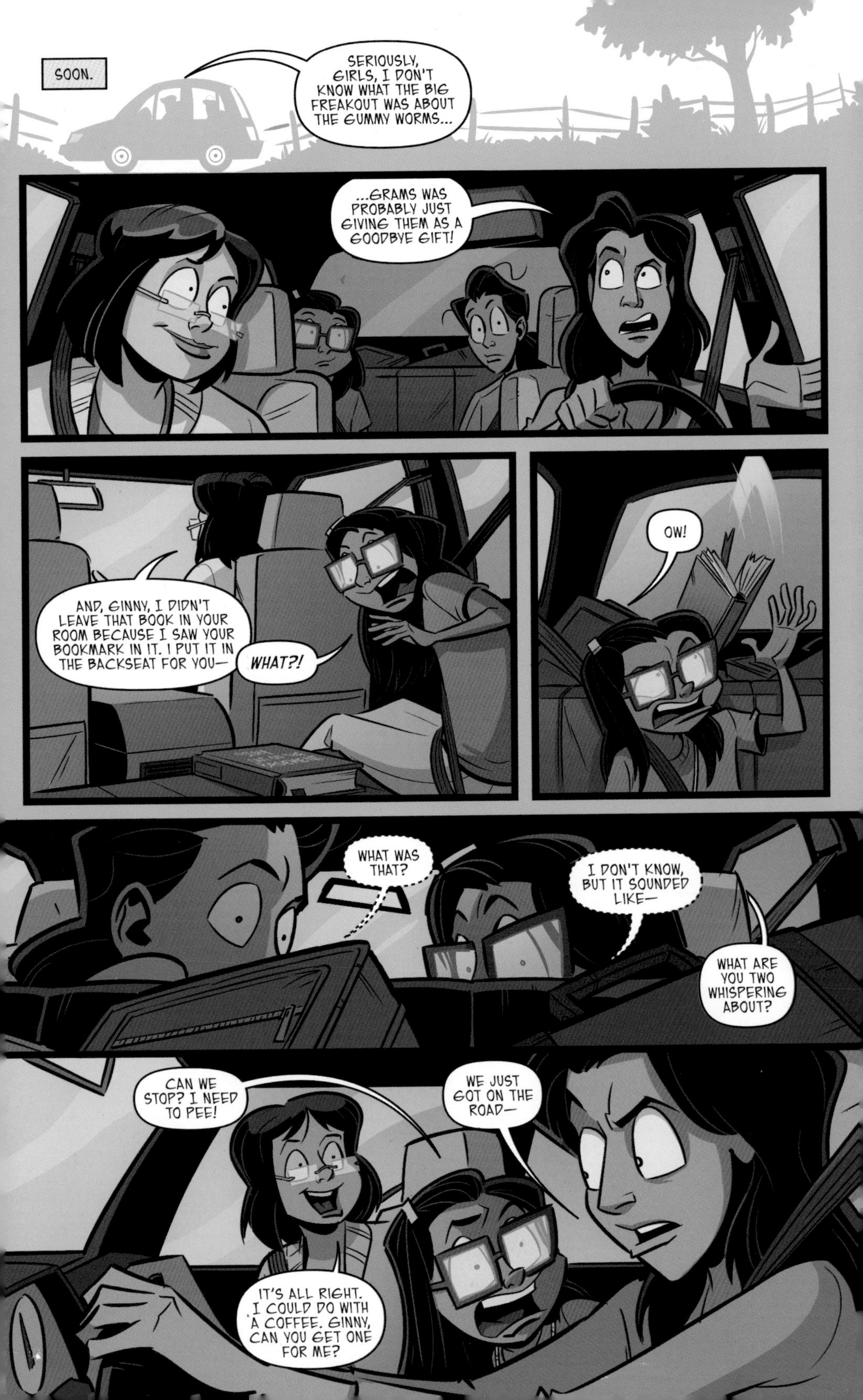
SOON.
SERIOUSLY, GIRLS, I DON'T KNOW WHAT THE BIG FREAKOUT WAS ABOUT THE GUMMY WORMS...
...GRAMS WAS PROBABLY JUST GIVING THEM AS A GOODBYE GIFT!
AND, GINNY, I DIDN'T LEAVE THAT BOOK IN YOUR ROOM BECAUSE I SAW YOUR BOOKMARK IN IT. I PUT IT IN THE BACKSEAT FOR YOU—
WHAT?!
OW!
WHAT WAS THAT?
I DON'T KNOW, BUT IT SOUNDED LIKE—
WHAT ARE YOU TWO WHISPERING ABOUT?
CAN WE STOP? I NEED TO PEE!
WE JUST GOT ON THE ROAD—
IT'S ALL RIGHT. I COULD DO WITH A COFFEE. GINNY, CAN YOU GET ONE FOR ME?

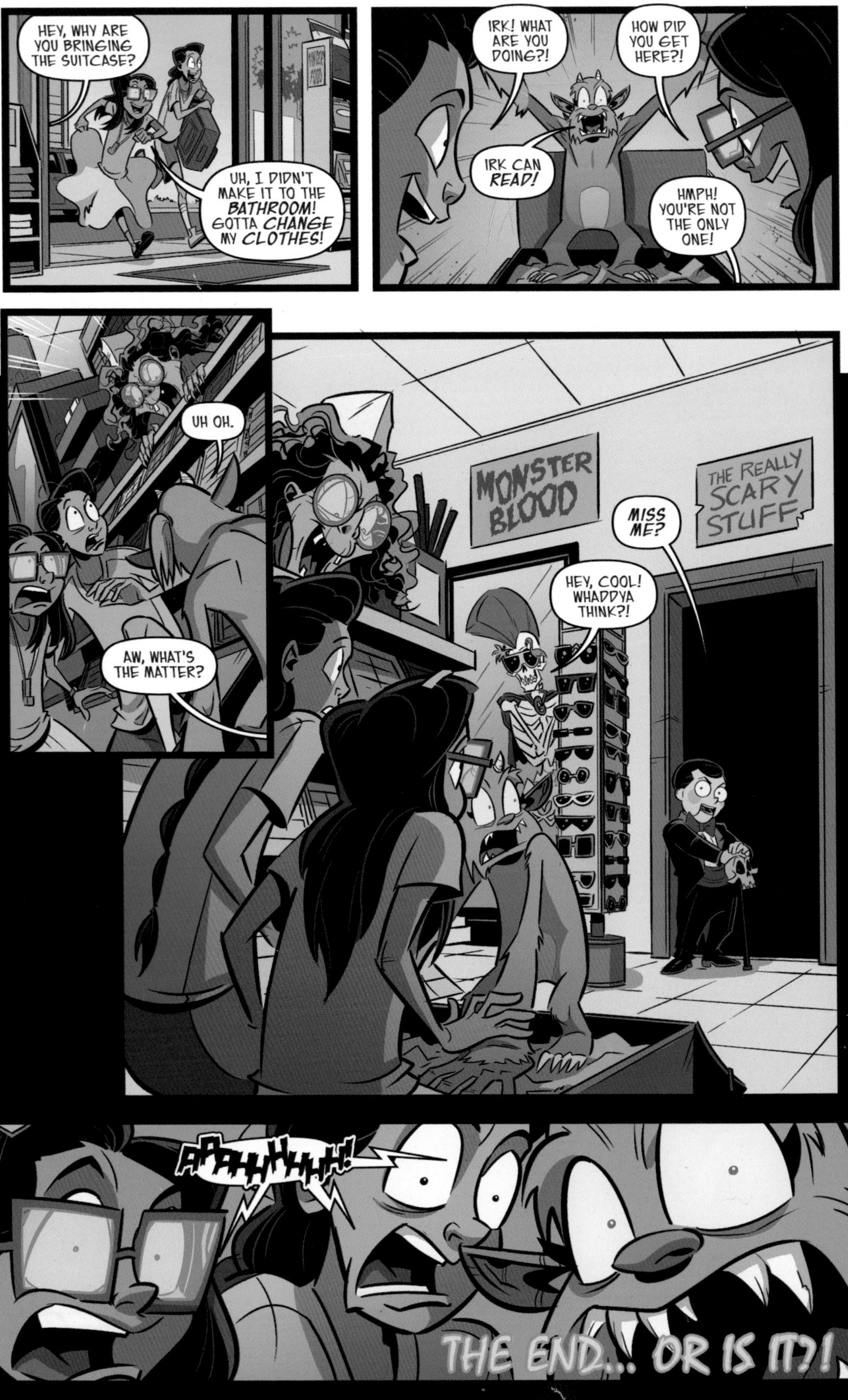
HEY, WHY ARE YOU BRINGING THE SUITCASE?
UH, I DIDN'T MAKE IT TO THE BATHROOM! GOTTA CHANGE MY CLOTHES!
IRK! WHAT ARE YOU DOING?!
HOW DID YOU GET HERE?!
IRK CAN READ!
HMPH! YOU'RE NOT THE ONLY ONE!
UH OH.
AW, WHAT'S THE MATTER?
MONSTER BLOOD
THE REALLY SCARY STUFF
MISS ME?
HEY, COOL! WHADDYA THINK?!
AAAHHHHHH!
THE END... OR IS IT?!

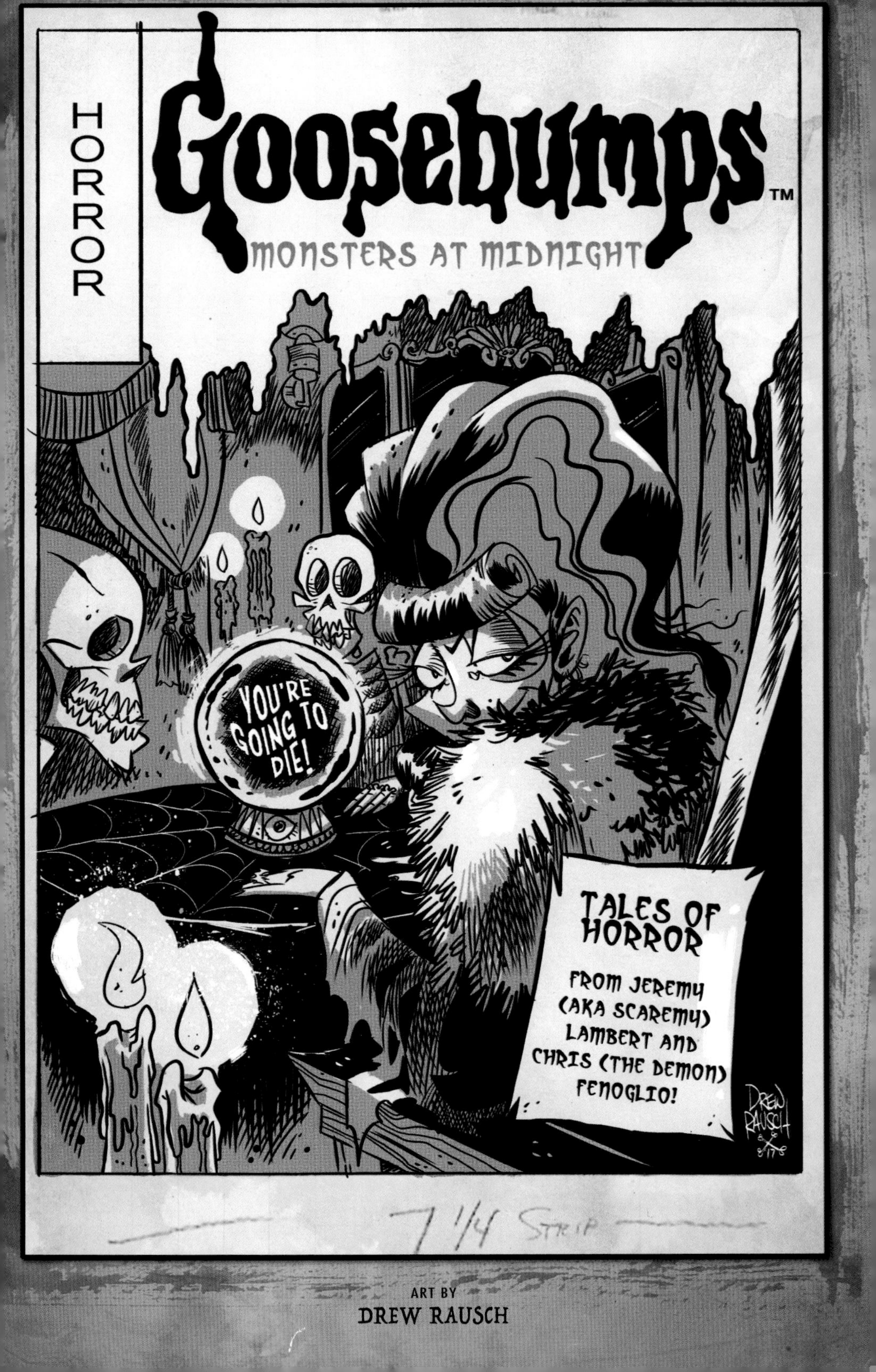
HORROR
Goosebumps™
MONSTERS AT MIDNIGHT
YOU'RE GOING TO DIE!
TALES OF HORROR
FROM JEREMY (AKA SCAREMY) LAMBERT AND CHRIS (THE DEMON) FENOGLIO!
DREW RAUSCH
7 1/4 STRIP

ART BY
DREW RAUSCH

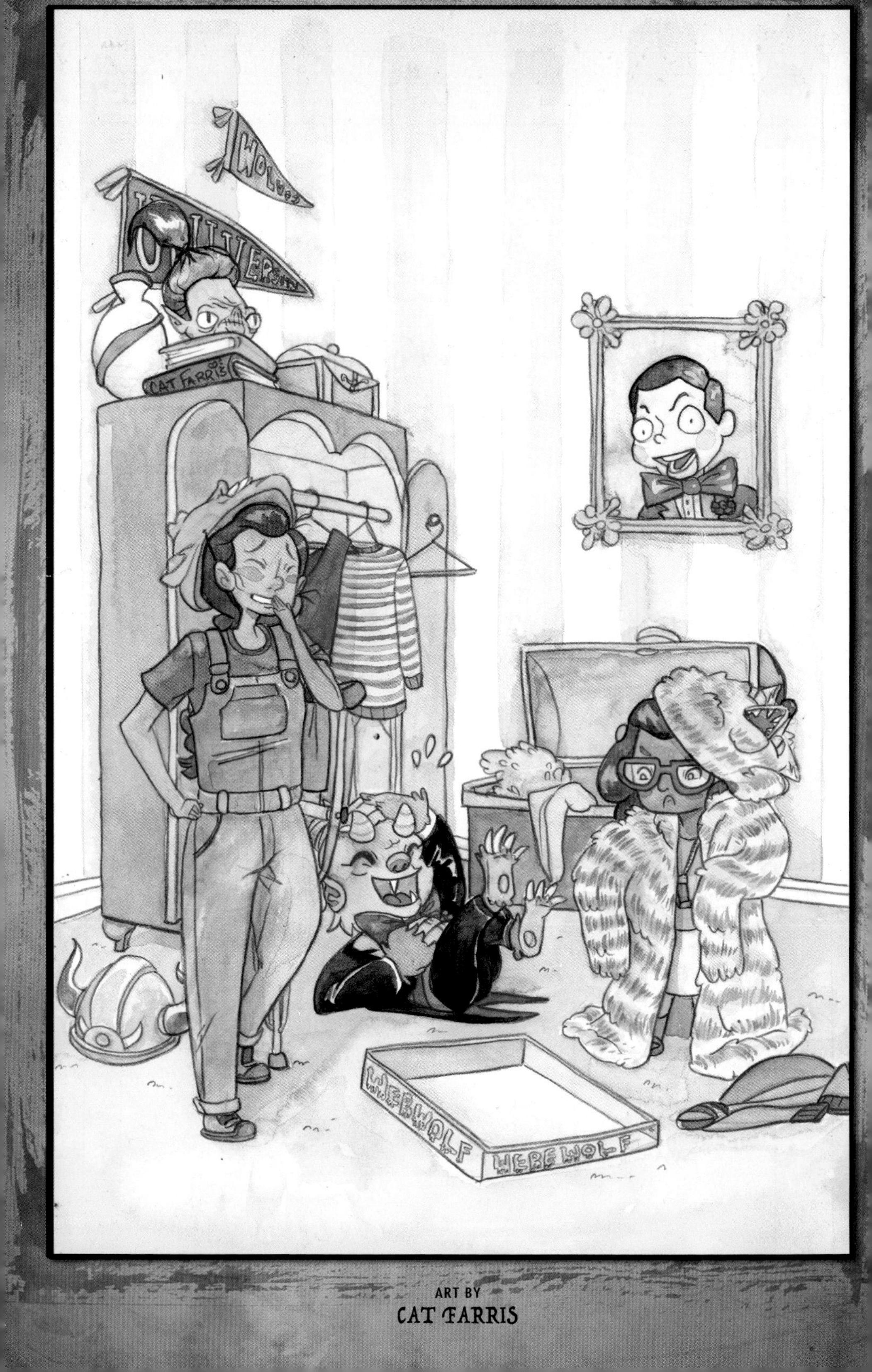
CAT FARRIS
WEREWOLF
WEREWOLF

ART BY
CAT FARRIS

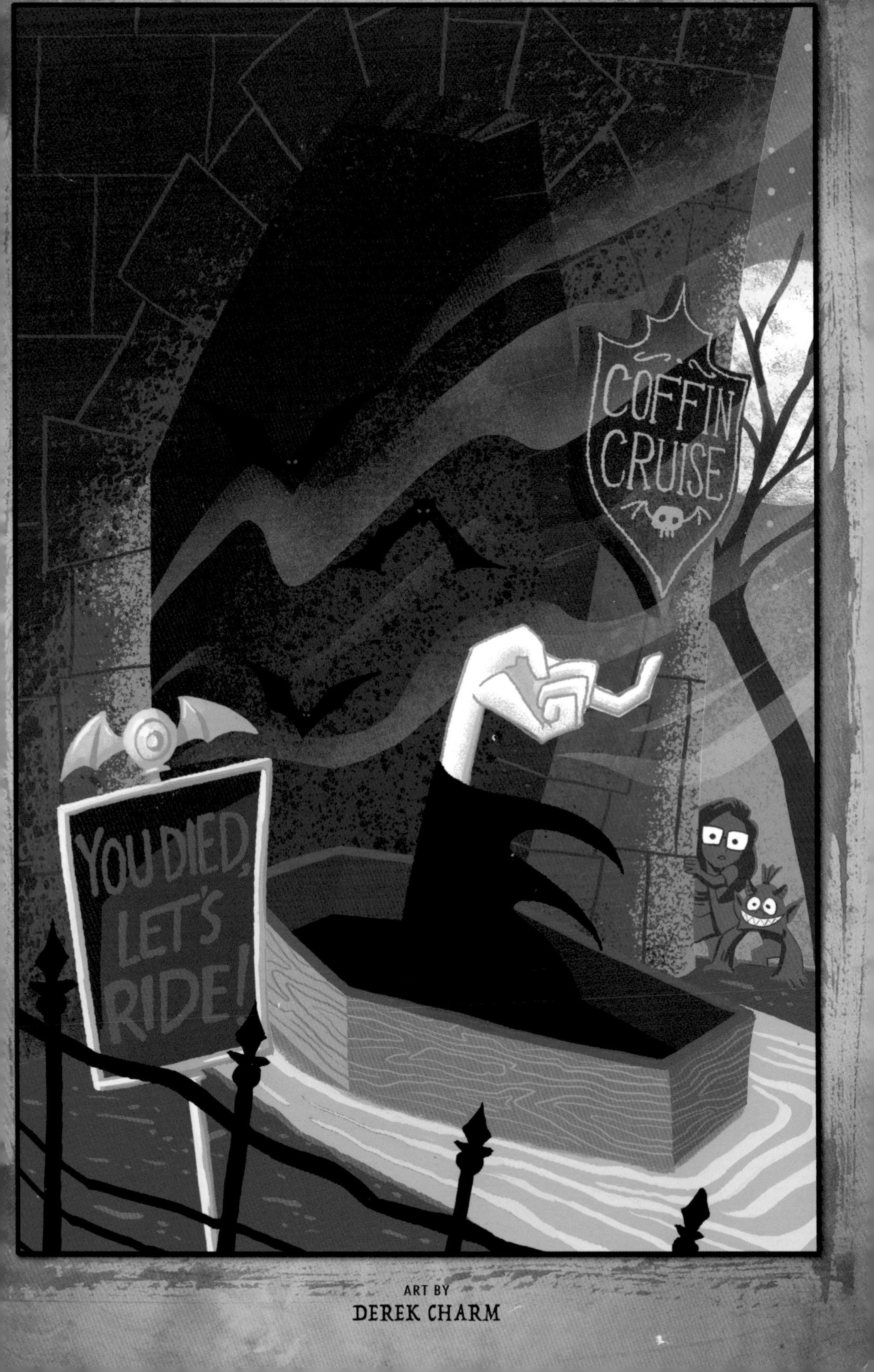
COFFIN CRUISE
YOU DIED, LET'S RIDE!

ART BY
DEREK CHARM

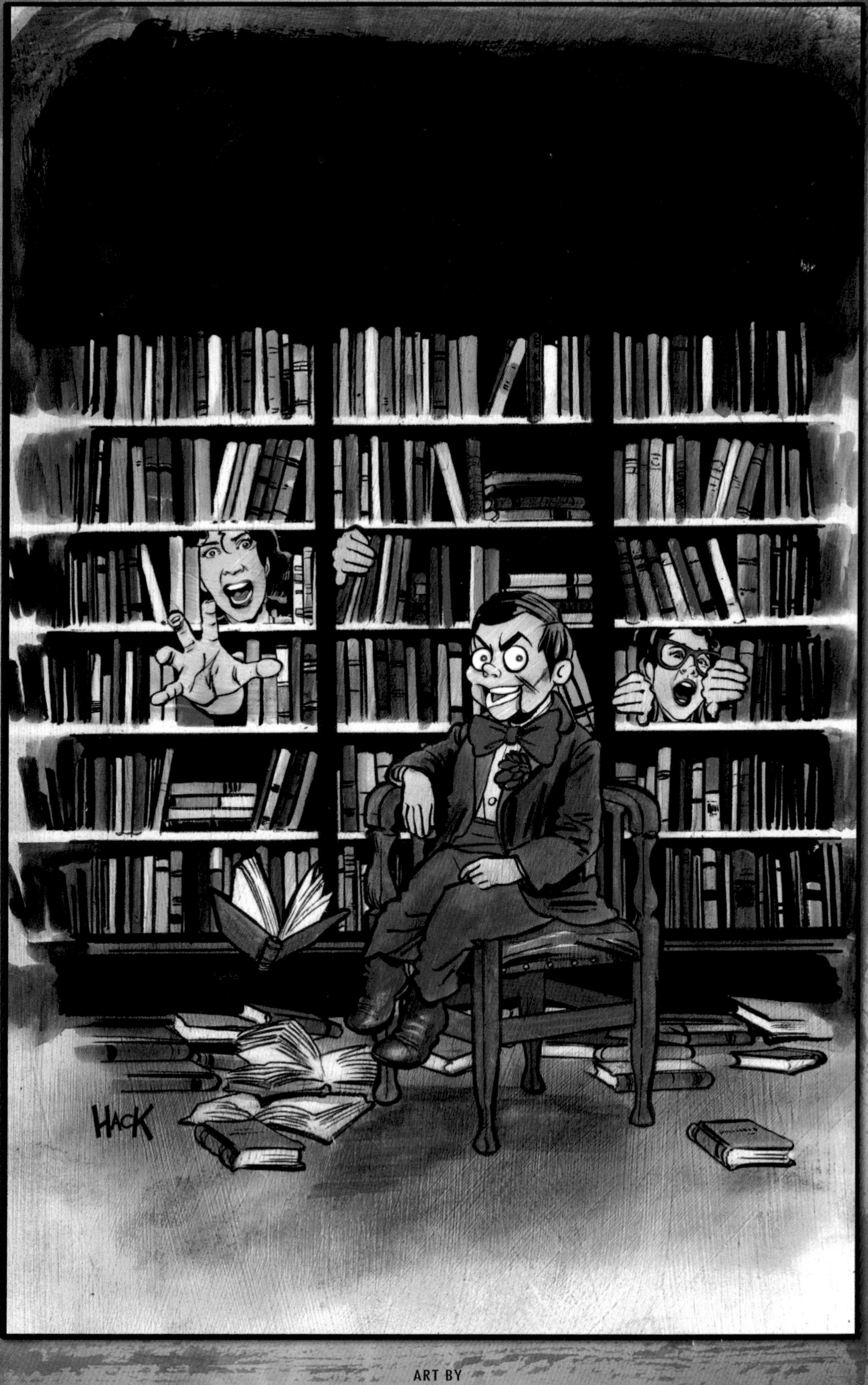
HACK

ART BY
ROBERT HACK